Come Tomorrow

by

Julian M. Miles

Published by Lizards of the Host Publishing
First edition, September 2013

This paperback ISBN: 978-0-9576200-5-6
Ebook (Smashwords Edition, multi-format) ISBN: 978-1-3014-5841-7

British Library Cataloguing in Publication Data. A catalogue record for this book is available from the British Library.

Design and layout by Julian M. Miles
Original front cover art by TLC Digital Art
Printed and bound in the UK by Inky Little Fingers

<u>Visit us online</u>
Julian M. Miles (a.k.a. Jae): www.lizardsofthehost.co.uk
Lizards of the Host Publishing: www.lothp.co.uk
Inky Little Fingers: www.inkylittlefingers.co.uk
TLC Digital Art: www.tlcdigitalart.deviantart.com

For Tina.

Because she trusted a stranger with one of her ladies.

Contents

Introduction: Here I Go Again

I have published two collections of flash and short science fantasy since becoming a staff writer for 365 Tomorrows (the web's premier science fiction, science fantasy and speculative flash fiction site). The initial flood of stories has settled to regular spurts of a half dozen or so pieces of flash and short fiction. I am inordinately lucky in that this creative process seems to be entirely independent of my day to day activities. A short fragment or concept springs to mind and the whole piece can emerge within an hour or two. I have learned to always review and correct it after a night's sleep, a simple habit that improves the quality of my work and makes my proof-readers' lives easier.

Someone once opined that flash fiction was limited by its brevity, that valid plots and topics would be swiftly exhausted. Hopefully I am gradually proving them wrong, but I shall let you be the judge of that.

So, on with my third venture in attempting to entertain, intrigue and inspire with the visions of futures and alternates that I have seen. I hope they are as edifying to for you read as they were for me to create.

Hacker

The pastel-decorated walls were hung with tasteful art that changed as needed to offset any negative morale the system garnered from the gestalt of everyone's mindnets. Since the advent of the cranial implant, society had changed beyond all recognition and this had forced policing to evolve as well.

Two figures leant against the wall of the hushed office, engaged in silent conversation like everyone else. Some predicted the death of all but the most rudimentary spoken language skills before the end of the century.

Detective Reid paused to put a datapad on the desk before resuming his conversation with Detective Constable Moore.

So we caught him at last?

Her. She's a basket case.

Given her hobby of vivisecting prostitutes, I'm not surprised.

No, not in that way. You know the transcriber purchase that originally flagged her?

Yes. Uniforms spotted it and we were following her for the regulation twenty-four hours before arrest. She went out killing that evening.

Seems that she did it deliberately so we would catch her.

What?

You need to listen to the transcriber. It's been verified.

The pair of them headed for the audience room and, in the presence of an evidence unit, the transcriber, an illegal device for undetectably recording mindnet chats, was set in playback mode.

We'll skip the early stuff, which includes the murder in full sensory pickup. It's the end you need to hear.

Moore gestured to the evidence unit. It cued and started the playback.

Her hysterical voice was shrill with emotive bias. She had bought a top of the line unit: "Oh god, oh god, oh god. No. No. I can't take this."

A second voice made Reid start. It was male. An exquisite old English accent reproduced with emotional tones of smug satiation.

"That's fine, Penelope. This was the last one for you. The police are on their way, they seem to have gotten wind of us. You can have your body back and remember: if you say anything about me they'll lock you up as a lunatic, because bodyjacking doesn't officially exist."

"But it wasn't me!"

"Of course it wasn't, Penelope. It was me. It has always been me. Now you lie down and they will be here to collect you soon. Sleep, dear Penelope."

"But I don't want to-"

Her voice became unintelligible as her consciousness was overridden. Reid turned to Moore, who raised a hand for him to wait and pointed at the transcriber.

"What follows is for the detectives listening to the transcriber that this clever filly bought to attract your attention."

Moore gestured for the evidence unit to pause the playback. He looked at Reid, who resorted to speaking, a stress-related habit of older people.

"Good god. We've got a slasher that hijacks normal people using their mindnets? ABM stock will tank if this gets out."

Moore shook his head before replying verbally out of politeness, his voice scratchy from underuse: "You're right. This one's going to be a huge mess. I thought you should hear the whole thing before an edited version becomes the official one."

Reid raised an eyebrow in query. Moore paused his gesture for the evidence unit to continue to ask: "What was District Seven before the Rezoning?"

Reid scratched his head then hunched as an ominous suspicion came with the answer: "Whitechapel."

Moore's shoulders slumped as he gestured to the evidence unit.

The smug voice seemed to fill the room: "Let this be the start once again. My name is Jack. Catch me if you can."

War Fare

My grandfather fought hardliners in Afghanistan, my father fought the Data Wars in India. Before them, every generation of my family had brought home a medal from a war somewhere. I only have my company badge.

Eight months ago I sat in an elegant office, where smoked chrome and softened leather clashed with multi-position display surfaces the size of my car. The man behind the desk was younger than me. His guns were on the wall and were shinier than mine. As I tried to read the titles on his certificates, his tone of voice changed and I paid attention now he'd finished the self-promotion.

"We're delighted that you want Mars Temperance to work with you on this action. Initial assessments prepared by our field teams for today's meeting show that a drone-led assault will minimise casualties and permit better scrutiny by United Nations monitoring, which is essential if the action is to be ratified as legal. There really should be no requirement for in-country teams from your nation whatsoever. The entire action can be resolved in full compliance without a single combatant being endangered on the ground."

My boss, Major-General Windlesham, smiled as he sat upright. "That's excellent news, Malcolm. You really think that we can pull this off without having to go through the invading force procedures?"

"Ninety-four percent certainty of resolution within two months without direct action, Major-General. The new monitored-warfare policies ensure that actions occur with a minimum of collateral casualties and the least investment of precious national manpower."

Three weeks into the "drone-led assault" the opposition bought their own drone servers online. Our fully-scrutinised and approved minimal collateral damage offensive became a shambles as they based their mobile control units in civilian areas. Their newly acquired multi-role drones outperformed ours. It only took a week to discover that while we'd gone to Mars-T they had gone to Hessian, the pioneers of guerrilla strategy-based counter-invasion operations. After a second massacre of innocents during an attempt to take out one of their control units, Mars-T were fired and I got a call.

I run a unique company in these console war days. They keep trying to retire us but things keep going out of bounds and we're needed. So they keep us on the payroll as Maintenance Group 22, a bolt-on of the spook divisions who are allowed to continue covertly as intelligence gathering is still deemed necessary.

Our job is simple. We find their drone control centres and anything else military, hidden and essential. Then we break them beyond repair. No scrutiny, no media, no quarter. Our paperwork may list us as MG22 and we'll never get any more medals, but it doesn't matter. Because our badge still reads 'Who Dares Wins'.

Big Brother

The battlefield is silent and empty. In the city beyond, we can see figures on the remaining vantage points. All of us gawking like children as the spectacle continues.

The dawning light reflects from angles or scatters in rainbow flashes across Sean's body which towers above the trees and is higher than most of the buildings in the city. With unbelievable grace, he executes a swooping lunge; his head briefly level with his ankles as his arms curve back and up, like wings spreading. The slipstream of his passing bends trees and flattens the few shanties they had supported.

"Colonel Jones, please instruct your brother to carry out his orders."

The voice in my earpiece is stiff with disapproval. This paradigm shift in warfare is beyond them.

"Brigadier Stephens. Major Jones is doing just that."

"Pardon me, Colonel. I had the silly idea that attacking a city involved fighting."

"Brigadier, you misunderstand me. I do not expect this city to fall."

"We don't have the men for a hundred and eighty square miles of urban combat, Colonel."

I see Captain Andrews raise a hand, his other one pointing at the white flag bobbing towards us from the city defences.

"Gentlemen, I expect hostilities to cease within the hour. Yes, Brigadier, I will resign before court-martial if I am wrong."

Sputtering over the earpiece is my only reply. After a while, the Captain arrives with our flag carrying visitor, who cannot take his gaze from my brother, even when he speaks.

Lieutenant Sprindi translates: "The humble representative of the people relays a request that when his august leaders capitulate, would the *dalishen* do them the honour of accepting their surrender in person?"

I smile at our visitor and switch to the command channel.

"Sean. Finish that pattern and get over here, will you?"

Sean finishes with a beautiful circling move, his hands moving so fast at its culmination you can hear the wind roar around them. After a simple bow toward the sun, he activates his gravtac and drifts our way, setting down with a gentle thud that only slightly demolishes our encampment. His feet are placed either side of the command tent. Our visitor is shaking like a leaf in the wind.

"Lieutenant, do tell the humble representative we agree before he faints."

A few moments later the representative is sprinting back to the city as Sean lets himself down carefully into a cross-legged sitting position. I lean against his toes until he extends a finger and gives me a boost to perch on his knee. I grin up into the immense sensor arrays so carefully designed to look like monstrous eyes.

"You were right. A two-hundred foot tall cyborg doesn't need weapons; it only needs to be invulnerable. The terror inspired by facing something that can swat aircraft by throwing tanks at them is stupefying. Your destructive potential is unthinkable and you devastate their morale just by arriving."

Sean chuckled over his speakers before resorting to command channel: "Good thing they needed the size to fit the first gravitic core. Sleight fields will keep me awesome until someone makes their own titans. Then things will get interesting."

"Which is why I recommend you add *Pehlwani* and *gada* to your *Wu-Shu*."

"Why?"

"They can't shoot you, so they'll take your lead. Seeing videos of your patterns, they'll select a striking art. Which will be utterly buggered by Indian wrestling and Hanuman mace."

"My big brother, still looking out for me. Love ya, Feargal."

I look up at him, my quadriplegic brother turned ad-hoc battlefield god: "I think the 'big' bit is yours now. Call me 'older'."

I see the watchers flinch as Sean's laughter roars out.

Momentary

I'm not in the moment. I am the moment, locked in by law-enforcement combat conditioning. Beyond my fixed perceptions, there is nothing. The instructors told us to take in the whole enhanced experience at these times, letting the moment become us instead of becoming our madness.

There's a nanopede traversing the barrel of my gun, its tentacular manipulators working devotedly to provide gecko-like traction in the sheen of tarnish-repellent gloss upon the burnished alloy. The legs move in waves, reflecting little coruscating showers of light as it makes its way about its incomprehensible business.

"One."

The stock of my gun is jammed tight into my shoulder, so tight my clavicle aches, but I can't diminish my grip. The sights are aligned to the probable target vectors and the filament to my combat eye swings rhythmically in time with my heartbeat. My peripheral vision shows my team and headman distributed for optimum coverage.

"Two."

The warehouse is silent. Our stealth gear means we are invisible even to Tabino, the plastic-addicted rodents famed for denuding citizens in moments. Thankfully the only citizens nearby are in the passing air traffic that illumines the darkness fitfully with bright beams through the torn roof. They strobe by like the strides of giants made of light.

"Three!"

The darkness is hurled back by the phased pulse of six demolition charges that turn air into energy with an efficiency that can suffocate the unprepared. Which is what we all hope our targets are. As the expanding rings of blue fire flash along exposed conductive materials, the bass thrum of a grazer amped from its work cycle of plasma cutting up to illegal death-dealing autopulse reveals some of our targets were very prepared.

My legs are a separate entity, hurling me forward on an irregular course. My sights show no targets yet the autopulses increase from one to eight, stretching out towards us like ribbons of purple light. They must be cycling the grazers without regard for cooling.

"I'm hit!"

One of the ribbons intersected with my headman and his right thigh has been blasted to superheated mist. Now I understand why they're running the grazers so hot – they can chop us down. I desperately try to find them, overriding the sights to fire at the originating end of the nearest lethal ribbon of light.

"Bastard!"

The scream over open comms coincides with the ribbon I was using to orientate my fire winking out. I'm just fighting my single-minded kill directive to rediscover speech, so I can pass the sight-override manoeuvre on, when two of the ribbons slash sideways and bisect in my chest, vapourising my forearms and detonating my gun. I watch in awe as the nanopede executes a flawless pike off the gun barrel and drops from view behind the expanding grey and silver ball of gun shards, denaturing chest armour and limb fragments. Then the physics happens and I am dropped off the impaling spears of energy, falling behind a thankfully solid stanchion.

The medical unit on my belt exhausts its entire repertoire in under five seconds. I am going to live, my arms, armour and weapon having reduced the death dealing beams to merely searing.

Released from combat mode, I open our tactical channel and tell my remaining team-mates about overriding their sights. Wordless grunts of thanks make me smile.

The moment stretches and snaps, normal time and senses are resumed and I manage to race the pain into the welcoming embrace of sedative oblivion.

The Art of Darwin

Sanderson's Paradise is a misnomer if ever there was one. A planet with nearly constant rain across immense supercontinents leaves you with two options for footing. Eroded mountain ranges where every indentation on the blue-grey landscape can become a river or plunge pool without warning; or swamp. The place has tropical swamps, frozen swamps and every class in between.

As a venue for war, it's a nightmare. Man just hasn't got over the need for fancy toys to do battle with. The first nine months were marked by the number of amphibious vehicles that became submerged coffins; the drowning gurgles of their occupants relayed all-too clearly over the tactical net. The damp ruined everything except fully environmentally sealed units. Which weapons, by their very nature, are not.

On top of the hostile terrain and weather, the locals are unimpressed with the two legged snacks that object so violently to being snacked on. This place has something that resembles an eight-legged alligator the size of a jumpship, with a bite that can crush armoured vehicles and press the juices out of all onboard. That's one of the obvious threats. The range of fungi, parasites, savage insects and randomly poisonous stuff is breathtaking.

A tour of duty here comes with a one in ten chance of leaving in the same state you arrived in. Needless to say, after the first year, the best of the best went to war elsewhere. As the costs escalated from over-budget to nigh-on unsupportable, we were sent the cheapest troops to fill our rosters: penal battalions, conscripts, death-wishers, all the fun people. And Takiri Anderson, an anthropologist with some of the last vestiges of aboriginal blood. He got sent here because he found out that antique boomerangs did not register on threat sensors as they spun in to fracture skulls. He chopped his way through half of the ruling council of Australia before they caught him.

He spent a couple of months floundering with everyone else, but after a year it was brought to my attention that he was enjoying himself and acquiring a bit of a reputation as a unit commander. So I called him in for a chat, just to give me a break from the constant demands to turn this expensive debacle into a victory or to find some palatable excuse to withdraw. The other side was apparently in a similar situation, but neither side wanted to lose face by being the first to retreat.

What presented itself at my door was a wiry man with very broad shoulders wearing only a cricket box that doubled as his weapon belt. He was clean, an unusual feature for those who spent nearly their entire non-sleeping existence at least knee-deep in mud.

"Good evening, Captain Salares. A pleasure to meet you at last."

"Mister Anderson. You seem to be the first person who likes it here. I'm curious as to why."

He smiled. It was genuine, but it made me nervous.

"I cannot tell you. But I will show you, if you dare. Meet me one after dawn at the eastern hatchway. Dress like me."

I pointedly looked down at the substantial assets that filled my uniform top.

He coughed as his face coloured. "I see. A combat brassiere would be a valid addition. Having one hand covering your legendary bust all the time would put you at a disadvantage. And be a crime."

My turn to colour up. But the implicit challenge piqued my interest.

"Very well, Mister Anderson. I shall see you there."

An hour after dawn and I arrived at the eastern hatch. Anderson was there, with a female colleague from his unit, who was skinny enough to not need a combat brassiere. As I got closer, I saw that she was actually naked except for a utility harness and field boots. Both had spears, neither had standard issue energy weapons.

Anderson did the introductions: "Captain Salares, Corporal Washington. One of my best students."

"Student of what?"

He grinned. "Of Sanderson's Paradise. I hope you too will appreciate what it has to teach us after today. Come on."

We exited the hatch and sprinted across the twenty metre stretch of quagmire into the jungle. As soon as we were amongst the huge trees, I was surprised by both of them leaping upwards, using vines and other growths with the ease of long familiarity. My determination not to be outdone was going to leave me with muscle strain tomorrow, but today I was not going to be shown up.

I had never been up to the canopy before. In fact, I could not think of anyone who had. Everyone regarded trees as obstacles. Deep-rooted monoliths to be cleared for operations to occur. I found myself amidst a plethora of green, blue and red leaves, walking along a branch wider than one of our personnel carriers. After rinsing off the mud from our sprint, using water from a pond that had formed in a hollow on a branch, we progressed rapidly, something unheard of to those who travelled across the sodden ground fifty or so metres below. Up here, the rain was warmer and the runoff cleaner. The creatures I saw were smaller. Down below, arachnids were armoured ambush predators. Up here, they were still big, but unarmoured, slimmer and prone to retreating at our advance.

Anderson suddenly froze in place and raised his fist. Washington and I tried our best to become statues. Moments later, a purple-furred mega-weasel appeared, sniffed Anderson and then passed us by without further indication that it cared about our presence.

As the violet crest on its tail disappeared from view, Anderson spoke quietly: “That is typical behaviour up here. There seems to be an ingrained live and let live policy. No unnecessary aggression occurs. Nothing fights for fun. More importantly, nothing has learned that we are foes. A couple of predators have decided we’re good eating, but they will only attack singletons. We have taught them that pairs and groups are too much to take on.”

I was silent as I took in this world above a world. We progressed at a brisk walking pace, at least six times faster than anyone on the ground could manage. After a good couple of hours, Washington exchanged whistling signals with unseen sentries and we climbed up into Anderson’s unit headquarters.

The sight before me was incredible. The crown of an ancient hardwood spread far, huge branches twining about each other with thigh-width vines wrapped about them. On this acre width expanse, Anderson’s unit had built a camp with a cooking range, personal quarters, armoury, command centre and everything a forward operating base could wish for. Everyone was either naked, or minimally dressed, except for harness. Everyone was armed with primitive melee weapons. I noticed that the perimeter sentries had racks of standard energy weapons. A quick mental count tallied with the unit strength. They kept all the high-tech stuff for defence.

Anderson came over to me. “This is how you should fight on Sanderson’s Paradise. From the comfort and safety of the canopy. We haven’t taken a casualty in the eight months since we moved up here. We’ve found plant extracts that counteract the fungal growths that like human flesh. Staying clean using local soapbark with the extracts mean we smell like we belong as well as being healthier. Trooper Michaels used to be a biochemist. He’s having a field day up here.”

I looked at his radiant smile. “That’s all very nice, but how about this war thing we’re actually here for?”

“Oh, that’s going well. We’re not much for one to one combat these days. It’s much easier to lure a mega-gator, an armadillo-roach pack or a swarm of tiger-wasps into enemy units and let them do the damage. They’ve declared this sector too dangerous to patrol, and are sure that we cannot get through it either. It’s flagged as a dead zone on their latest command maps.”

I started. Getting intelligence like that was incredibly rare.

“Oh, it’s quite easy to drive the predators off. We’ve just about compiled a complete list of what runs away from what down below. So we drive the attack beasts off and descend to pilfer the wreckage and finish off any survivors with weapons made from local materials. Nothing to hint that their enemy is involved. By the time they come back on a rescue and salvage run, the local scavengers have hidden our handiwork.”

The man was a bloody genius! Guerrilla warfare using the local environment. But he'd been doing this for months. Why hadn't he reported?

Anderson had been watching me. He raised a palm to me: "I didn't report our success because my unit is in agreement with me. Sanderson's Paradise is just that to us. We want formally recorded claim to live here autonomously after the campaign ends. We can provide a wealth of useful trade items to support our status as an independent planet beholden to our side."

"Trade items?"

"Like I said, Michaels is a biochemist. Corporal Daguerre is a herbalist. This place is like a vast store of new ingredients to them. I can provide you with samples of their first little discovery, just to add weight to the deal."

This convict soldier was trying to bargain with me?

"We have the cure for McCormick's Disease."

He looked at me as I paled and staggered backwards to sit on something. His face showed concern, not glee. He didn't know. But I knew he and his tribe-cum-unit would get my full backing for their claim. In fact, I could ratify the damn thing. A convict's sentence was one campaign. This campaign was going to go from a life sentence to a resounding victory damn quick, I was now sure.

"My daughter has McCormick's. My husband took early demob to care for her."

Anderson sunk down into a cross-legged position. He actually looked apologetic.

"Oh, I am sorry. That really wasn't fair. I would have offered one of the other remedies had I known, you must believe that."

I was surprised to find that I did.

"How advanced is she?"

"Second phase, held at bay by daily micro-laser treatments, rigorous protein supplementation and steroid backed forced muscle replacement."

Anderson shouted out: "Daniel! Second phase McCormick's stalled by muscle overgrowth and pruning! That's one of those immersion cases you were chatting about, isn't it?"

A blacker than night chap with brown eyes jogged over.

"That's right, Takiri. Sooner the better and here. We can use the hyper-water springs as a base for the solution."

Anderson turned back to me.

"Get your daughter and your husband here as soon as you can. He'll be needed to care for her until she's recuperated, because we have a war to win."

There was no doubt in his eyes. None at all. Even if there had been, I could not risk turning down a chance for my girl.

"How long?"

"She'll need to be fast-transited. Daniel; sorry, Trooper Jeffries will need access to your daughter's medical records to make up recommendations for pre-flight booster treatments and palliative care during the trip. Once she's here we can get her in a bath that should stop the whole thing in oh, hang on. Daniel?"

"Worst case, terminal end of phase two should be clear within a month. After that, it's recuperation. If she was a vigorous kid before infection, six months living up here would be best. Oh, it would be handy to not have a war going on."

I stared into his guileless smile in the grip of a burgeoning hope that I never thought to feel. I had started this day determined not to betray myself in front of the troops. Now I sat in a growing ring of genuinely caring faces, crying my eyes out.

In between sobs of hope, I looked about and finally returned my tearful stare to Anderson.

"I presume that you selected your unit carefully from those on offer, picking those who would integrate best?"

"Of course."

"Then I will give you access to the profiles of all personnel on this planet. Pick the ones that will bring your colony up to strength."

Everyone acted like they had been electrified. My use of the word 'colony' had not been missed. I grinned fiercely.

"The forces under my command are now assisting Takeshi's Hope, the newly-recognised sovereign colony of Sanderson's Paradise, to defend itself from an erroneous incursion brought about by poor intelligence gathering. I will quietly inform those who need to know what you have on offer. A colony with such revolutionary treatments can get backing and funding for damn near anything. A penal battalion bargaining for somewhere nice to live have sod all chance."

Blaming flawed reconnaissance data would allow both sides to cease operations and pull out with no embarrassment.

There were tears and muted cries of disbelief. Anderson just sat like a man thunderstruck.

"Governor Anderson, you're going to need to appoint staff. My husband would be an excellent liaison between the colony government and my military. What say you?"

Washington kissed his cheek, slapped the back of his head, then wrapped her arms around his shoulders and looked at me with tears running round her smile: "He thinks that is an excellent suggestion, but apologises for suddenly needing to lie down for a while."

The Accidental Godling

George stood on the fused glass at the edge of the crater. It had taken him a while to climb out of the hole, but at least it allowed the forces arrayed against him to reassemble. He watched them advance, flicking his eyes between reality and nihil, fascinated that living organisms produced a shadow in that non-place.

A thought came to him. With thought came actuality and he flickered to all perceptions except his own, a curious moment when he briefly ceased to be, then returned. In the command and control centre thirty miles away, consternation erupted as Major-General McChase keeled over, dead before his body started to fall.

George felt elation. Another thing learned. He could nullify the nihil shadow of an organism and the organism itself died instantly. With a rush of curiosity, he flickered a thousand times, nullifying the nihil shadows of things ranging from plankton to trees to whales. On his return to his standing place, he could sense the absences he had created. So he had proven shadows and echoes in nonexistence. But could it be nonexistence if he was there to see things?

His fascinated theoretical conjuring was interrupted by a massively amplified voice.

"Professor George Andrakoplis. This is Acting Commander Lamont. Surrender yourself for detention!"

Plainly as incapable of understanding as his predecessor. Maybe the next one? He flickered.

"Ack!"

The amplified noise of fatal surprise echoed. So his absences were infinitesimal in time consumption? Probably zero in real terms. He chuckled. 'Real terms'. Now there was a phrase he couldn't use anymore.

He paused his mental dissertation to gauge the approaching forces. He extended his newly acquired sense of hadronic potential over them and laughed to himself as he did so. Of course none of them had a large hadron collider with a gap just big enough for him to fit into, to separate him from the nihil with racing neutrons, to turn him into a four dimensional entity again, to have the proton stream inflict another unpredictability upon him. Most likely it would actually end him, instead of a further freakish transformation.

He raised a hand to his forehead as an epiphany struck him. His sudden movement caused the entire advancing army to grind to a halt and dive for cover.

Could it be dark matter? He hadn't been gifted with the ability to cease to be; he had been given access to the cloth upon which the tapestry of existence hung. Like any embroidery, he should be able to discover how to unpick bits of it.

He looked up as contrails laced the sky. How apt. Lacework. He cocked his head as cries of consternation echoed from the ranks arrayed before him. The missiles were not of their sending. It looked like an opportunist nation was using the situation to try to deal with him and their opposition in one holocaust.

Well, he had a theory. What better time to practice than with something that should allow him to shift the perceptions of those before him? He flickered, disappeared, flickered and generally reinforced the fear of the unknown amongst those watching him. Minutes later he reappeared and stayed. The nuclear armageddon rained down in a series of solid impacts and detonator-sized blasts, but not a mushroom cloud rose nor did a Geiger counter twitch.

He smiled, spread his arms and shouted: “Now can you get past your terror so we can talk like rational beings?”

Perks

The hump of mud hides a dreadnought. I hit it at over two hundred kay and launch into a barrel roll with a twist, dropping on the front left wheel. My compensator system spins the wheel hard so it skids away from the impact instead of folding the axle. I crash down inverted and pucker up as the cockpit rolls in three axes to point my eyeballs where my ride is going.

An elated whoop is followed by Sarge's voice: "Goddamn, son. You only lost thirty kay and we got the airtime against the moon. Money shot, boy."

"Cheers, boss. Where's Scrap Two?"

"Gully running in Sector Four. Trying to set a new record. The buy-ins are in six figures."

"That's because gully running is killtime, Sarge. Get Lara outta there."

A fatality would bring unwanted attention. More importantly, I don't want to lose my sister.

We're the Strategic Recovery Group, "dedicated teams of brave specialists who restore landscapes damaged in this tragic war" as the reporter who fell head over heels in lust with Sarge said in his report for SolNet. It was such a glowing review we got a free hand to carry on as we were.

Most of the planets left after a campaign are ruined. Poncing about with landscape gardening on a continental scale takes too long. We use a combination of liquefactors and neutraliser nanotech. When the place ain't toxic anymore, we drop florabombs and nanogardeners, then bugger off. Faunapods land five years later if the flowers have taken, otherwise its sterilisation and start again. Three years after the creatures land, United Planets auctions off the colonisation rights.

They actually make a huge profit. We get next to nothing, so we're creative about making ends meet. The scrappers are dreadnought-framed single-driver monsters with spherical wheels at each corner, powered by a gravitic drive core in each wheel. The ultimate no-roaders. We have three, all built from salvage. Two run on each planet, with the whole experience shown live on GhostNet. Survival time betting, stunt betting, sheer insanity manoeuvres betting, we get a cut of it all.

"Scrap One, Scrap Two, recall recall recall. Possible inspector incoming. Move it!"

SRG inspectors were notorious for being ex-regular-army bastards with a love of bureaucracy and a resounding contempt for us 'war-chasers'.

By the time I had parked and cleaned up, the visitor was ensconced in the meeting room. As I walked in, I got to see the tail end of my spectacular roll in glorious hi-def on the vidwall. The inspector, a young woman with no bust and hair barely qualifying as a suedehead sat watching, her face expressionless. I also saw that she wasn't an inspector. Her badges translated to SRG Captain, previously Armoured Recon, with three valour awards above the campaign patches that ran down her sleeve out of sight. A veteran madbuggy rider, transferred to SRG for what?

She looked up as I entered. Her eyes were ruby lensed prosthetics, her voice crisply British: "Corporal Jamie Danvers. Brother to Lara, who is currently costing us money being rescued from the gully collapse she caused."

She raised a hand as my concern showed. "She's fine, Danvers. But you really need to teach her about groundwave resonance. Now sit."

I did.

"I'm your new head girl: Captain Elaine Fleming. I requested this posting, because apart from allegations of equipment misappropriation, you are the best."

She grinned.

"I can see that your scramblers are cannibalised from wrecks. That squashes the allegations, leaving only one question before I'm happy."

I looked at Sarge. He shrugged. We looked at her.

"When do I get mine?"

Food Chain

Imagine a blue spider. One of the big hairy ones that move really fast. Make it the size of a tomcat. Replace the back pair of legs with bat wings. Add venomous spurs to those wings. That's what is watching me as I sway head-down in the breeze that wafts through the Ghabeni forest.

It's called a Darth. The wheezing noise they make when angered is the reason for the name and only dead biologists know why. They're pack hunters occupying the ecological niches usually taken by small carnivores, large rodents, small raptors, all sizes of scavenger and scary ginormous insects.

I inherited my father's arachnophobia in full measure. All I can focus on is what those legs will feel like against me when it climbs down the harness that suspends me from this tree like some macabre bird feeder.

When the orbiter malfunctioned, we abandoned it in the shuttle. When the shuttle malfunctioned, we abandoned it using parawings. They worked perfectly apart from the lack of open ground to land on. So we had a shouted discussion, slowed to stall speed while getting as low as possible, then dropped into the trees.

I can see Angus' red suit from here. He stopped screaming a while back but his suit is still moving. The type of movement that makes me think Angus is lunch for the rest of the Darth pack.

I don't even have a bright light to repel them. That's their only real aversion, apart from the nocturnal predator we have no name for as it's never been recorded. We've found entire Darth packs reduced to scattered chitin, every piece showing signs of powerful pointy teeth. The owners of said teeth remain a mystery.

A vibration on my harness makes me look up. In the creeping twilight, I see movement on the branches above. Looking across at Angus, I see his suit hanging like it's empty. Oh crap.

There's a Darth on my boot chewing on the laces, another going through the panels on my leggings. More are coming down the harness toward my boots. This is going to be a bad way to go, eaten from the feet up. I don't scream until I feel mandibles pierce my calf. Then I spend a few minutes making up for lost time until I feel legs moving down my inner thigh, under my suit. I piss myself, hit a new high note and pass out.

I come to, tasting blood. There are no mandibles in me, no legs on me. A crunching draws my eyes to the nearby branch. There is light from a crude lantern. In it I see that I am being observed by silvery oval eyes set slantwise in a head that strikes me as a cross between chimpanzee and leopard. The body is covered in dark blue fur, the hands and feet have six digits, two being opposable and the other four having wicked claws. The mouth is filled with sharp incisors. It licks the last morsels from the Darth carcass and throws it over its shoulder.

Far to my left, I hear the click of scanners. It looks in that direction and uncoils the prehensile tail it was sitting on to pick up the lantern.

"Thank you."

I don't know what prompts me to say it, but I do. The creature leans close, touching my cheek with a single clawless digit. I swear it smiles as it pats it's obviously stuffed belly. I realise the meaning: it didn't save me, it just can't eat anymore. With that, it extinguishes the lantern and is gone silently in an eyeblink.

As the rescue team approaches, it's not fear of Darths that makes me scream.

Life Star

The room was smoky with the singed emissions of substances that made tobacco seem like a health supplement. Everyone knew the risks, but when you were fighting the greatest tyranny to ever rule humanity, longevity just didn't enter the equation.

General Pantoro couldn't believe what he had heard: "We're sure about this?".

Intel Captain Lokus smiled: "It's confirmed, sir. The damn thing has no defensive field generators and no trace of fusion armour."

Major Ekrofan raised a fist: "Then we should strike against – what did you say Una Galacta had named it?"

Lokus checked his brief before replying: "Torush One."

Ekrofan laughed: "Bloody silly name."

All assembled looked to the General. Pantoro pondered for a moment, then nodded decisively: "Let's take their new toy away. Tell the Antares and the Ceres that they are cleared for nuclear engagement."

The twin battlecruisers Antares and Ceres approached the near lunar-diameter sphere that hung in equidistant orbit between Earth and Mars. They were heavily cloaked and relying on the chaos created by their attack to give them time to escape, accepting the fact that they might have to go down fighting. It was worth the sacrifice. Torush One was constructed of an unknown element, silvery-white with sections of mirror-like reflectivity. Una Galacta had noticeably decreased military operations since it had arrived in orbit, probably from the regime's fabled hidden construction facility. Which indicated how overwhelming they thought it would be.

In the smoky room, a communications officer approached the General. He whispered to Pantoro, whose brow creased as he entered a secure comms booth. The conversation he had was short and he exited the booth with a look of terror on his face. He rushed to the main comms board: "Abort the attack! Stand down all combat units! Stop! Just stop!"

Antares fired first. The damn thing was so big, missing was not the issue. Everyone agreed that all the nukes had to land dead centre to rip their way to the heart of it. With a ripple in space, the Ceres appeared and unleashed her payload. The ships used every nuke the Resistance could muster.

General Pantoro sat and cried. No one could get a word of sense from him.

Antares and Ceres linked their comms:

"I've got nothing on detectors. Not one hostile or countermeasure against the nukes or us."

"Confirmed, we seem to have caught them napping."

"Hang on; I have surface geometry variance from the target."

"No impacts yet. What's the cause?"

"Unknown. There's a dimple forming in the centre."

"A what?"

"A crater. Right where we've targeted. It's getting deeper and the rate is accelerating."

"Do you get a bad feeling about this?"

"Yes. Disengage and get the hell out is my instinct."

"Agreed."

Torush One flowed into itself, the crater sinking far enough to become a tunnel as Torush One changed from a sphere to a torus. The nuclear hopes of the Resistance passed cleanly through the hole, hurtling toward Earth where automated defences destroyed them.

Pantoro looked up, his face ashen: "It's not their superweapon. It's an intergalactic arbiter, sent to end the futile war we're engaged in and the tyranny we fight. Una Galacta will become a benevolent leadership under threat of unstoppable annihilation."

The room erupted with cries of "Victory!"

The General stood slowly: "No. Una Galacta ceased hostilities and delayed informing us so we would think that Torush One was theirs, make a desperate attempt to destroy it and in so doing, contravene the ceasefire. We will be liquidated for that. Una Galacta regard 'last man standing' as an acceptable win."

Brother Messiah

Jeremy huddled in the darkest corner of the cellar as the bombs rained down. Dust sifted from the ceiling as the concussions shook the foundations of the old house.

After an interminable time, the raid ceased and the sonics resumed, consisting of a single sentence, endlessly broadcast at two hundred decibels: "Give us back our god!"

The scientific expedition to Marduk III had brought back a single specimen, a unique hyper-intelligent telepathic creature which resembled a tiny winged seahorse and called itself 'Frem'.

The mission report stated that there had been a 'misunderstanding' with the Marduka over this creature. In the end, the expedition had evacuated under heavy fire.

On the way to earth, the scientists had bickered amongst themselves over time with Frem. This escalated into violence, so their escort took charge of it. Guard duty roster arguments resulted in the captain of the escort, Jeremy's brother, taking charge of Frem.

Jeremy had been woken by Julian collapsing in his hallway. As he was realising that his brother had been fatally shot, a questing thought touched him and a tiny head rose from his brother's fist.

He wants you to look after me. He is sorry he cannot talk but his body is past functional limits. He says he loves you and that you'll know what to do. You need to run now.

Jeremy did, grabbing his go-bag and Frem before torching his home. By the time the authorities had finished sifting the ashes, he was gone; all traceable gear dumped down a drain while leaving town over rough ground on a mountain bike.

He disappeared into the wilds, finding refuge deep in the Ozarks.

In an abandoned farmhouse, Jeremy chatted with Frem. It was during one of those chats he followed a hunch and Frem admitted that it was a construct. An information device created centuries before to record the inhabited universe in fluid crystalline pico-matrices until Frem attained a certain state of readiness. Taking everything in, sifting and discarding the phenomenal amount of duplication, Frem had details of the very best of everything ever created by intelligent life.

Jeremy's brother had hooked Frem up to the worldnet just after they landed. It had taken Frem less than an hour to get everything it wanted while ignoring every security precaution out there, not bothering to hide its presence.

While Julian went AWOL with Frem despite being shot, a global security crisis escalated as every side realised all their secrets had been stolen. They knew the location of the servers that the attack had originated from. In an alliance of mistaken desperation, they turned on the USA. Retaliation and desperate defence invoked World War Three.

Into this apocalypse descended the Marduka. They had worshipped Frem for a century or so and their learning during that time gave an advantage that was unassailable. After defeating Earth's military, the Marduka turned to getting their oracle back. When investigations got nowhere, they resorted to terror. The Earth would be bombed until Frem was returned.

Down in the corner of the cellar, Jeremy eased his conscience by believing in Frem.

They will give up soon, thinking me lost in the nuclear exchanges they arrived too late to nullify. When they are gone, we can start.

That was why Jeremy hid while billions died. Because Frem was finally ready. It had enough information to guide any level of civilisation into becoming a utopia beyond any that had ever existed.

Jeremy and Julian had always loved the idea of a new start, frequently discussing how to fix the world long into the night. To honour his brother's memory, Jeremy would see it through. With Frem, he knew he could succeed.

End of Days

The sun filled nearly a quarter of the sky. The lowest edge had just touched the horizon when Junella smiled and pointed toward it, her far-sight discerning something before the other observers yet again.

Eventually the silhouette of a man walking with a pronounced limp became visible. The observers stood with their weapons ready until they could see the colours on his Stetson. Then they relaxed, exchanging rapid sarcasms in the dialect Junella did not understand. She knew they did it deliberately.

Lamarat limped into camp, dustier than before, his face drawn and eyes tired. His smile belied his exhaustion, spreading wide and warm as Junella stood to offer him some water. He raised his offhand in a time-honoured insult toward the observers as he drank without pausing for breath.

As the sun set, Junella stoked the fire and stirred the broth. Finally she settled across from Lamarat, passing him a bowl with half of the broth. He looked at the size of the portion, then up at the observers.

"They excommunicated you?"

"Warben got his way and the tribe is his. I hear they have not eaten meat since."

"What's a little deprivation if you can control the tribe? I presume he excommunicated me as well?"

She smiled at him: "Of course. You are far too good at doing everything he struggles at."

He grinned right back: "Plus we share this heresy that the sun is baking the Earth to death."

"The black henges are the only source that tells of the sun getting hotter. The sacred stones and worship tablets tell of angels, demons, giants, gods, risen dead and great battles. I feel the heat drying the land yet I see no hosts."

"So you still do not regret us?"

Junella smiled at him. So strong in everything except believing he was the beat for her heart: "I regret only that those who carved the black stones did not fulfil their promise to return in the final days, to give the descendants of those who chose faith over science the same choice."

Lamarat rose and stepped round the fire to her, secrets dancing in the flames reflected in his eyes. Taking her hands, he raised them to his lips, then stepped away holding only one of her hands, as if to start a dance. He pointed toward where the sun had set.

"Two days west is the plain of the black henges. Resting upon those monoliths is a spaceship like I had only seen in the murals that show the Exodus of the Sinners."

His flicked his hand and instead of the knife Junella expected, there was a short baton resting on his palm.

"They said they would come for me as they left unless I called to turn their offer down. They understood my need to come back and ask you."

She placed her hand over his.

"Let us go together to meet our new tribe. This one has done with us and keeping our new family waiting would be impolite."

A Matter of Scale

"Our seventy-first attempt was successful, General. We have managed to intercept one of the filaments."

"Excellent news, Newman. Now tell me why you look worse than you did yesterday."

"Because the filament yielded some surprises."

"Surprises?"

"It's better if you see, sir."

The two men exited the room and walked down a short corridor and through an airlock. In the room beyond were a group of scientists who seemed to be in varying stages of shock, standing around a small table with an atmospherically-sealed dome over it. Newman waved everyone aside and gestured the General toward the table.

"As you know, the filaments appeared five years ago. First the news called them 'grey threads'. Then the filaments started going through people. Millimetre-wide holes through you will at best be excruciatingly painful, at worst fatal. Panic started to spread until my colleague, James Leon, discovered resonant deflectors. From there, we moved on to containment and prevention. Earlier today, we succeeded. What we wanted was to get a sample of these filaments. What we got was what was *inside* the filaments. Take a look. Use the magnifying lens."

The General moved closer. He looked through the lens and recoiled: "What the-?"

"It's a spaceship, sir. Rather advanced, but minute. We can even hear them, after slowing them a bit and running them through a translation program."

"We can translate their language?"

"We can, but only because it is a root language of Albanian."

"Good grief. That's one for bigger brains than ours. Proceed."

Newman stepped forward and pressed a button marked 'speakers'. A clamour of voices filled the air. As all present leaned in attentively, two voices rose above the hubbub.

"Svensang, you said these new routes were safe!"

"They are, for all that they cut through a section of subspace that we haven't used before. Since we started five years ago, freight has been moving through without incident. The savings in transit time are huge. We've paid for the project twice over. But this, this is unprecedented."

The General turned to Newman: "Can we communicate with them?"

"We can, but quite frankly it would probably be fruitless. They seem to have a slightly more bureaucracy-bound world government, while their only scientific advance over us is this 'subspace' travel."

"Why is it under a dome?"

"Mainly so we know where it is. Imagine a fly with tiny nuclear missiles, if you will."

"Point taken. Now set up a device that lets me shout at them. Not literally, but I need it to be loud."

Newman looked puzzled but did as ordered.

The General drew his automatic and gestured to the dome: “Lift it so I can slide my hand under it.”

When that had been done, the General slid the hand holding the gun under the edge, then drew the microphone closer with his other hand.

“Now hear this, all personnel on the - ?” He looked at Newman.

“World Battleship Nineteen.”

“All personnel on World Battleship Nineteen. Your subspace is our real space and you are becoming a nuisance. Stop using this section of subspace immediately. If you do not, the consequences will be serious. Please note the object that has entered your proximity.”

With that, he moved the nozzle of the pistol slowly up to the vessel, waggled it and then withdrew it and his hand from the dome.

Over the speakers, sounds of confusion persisted for about five minutes. Then the same two voices came to the fore.

“That was a gun barrel. Held in a hand. Scale it, treating this ship as one unit in length, Svensang.”

“That would make the gun nine units long with a bore of half a unit. The being grasping it has a hand length of six units, meaning the holder is about sixty units tall, if their average proportions match ours.”

“Then if their technology matches ours except in scale, they will have missiles the diameter of our planet.”

“Yes, Director.”

“Return using a vector that exactly reverses our entry route. No deviance. I am guessing they will allow us that.”

The General nodded to Newman, who gestured for all recording and sensor equipment to be readied.

With a grey-blue flash and an audible pop, World Battleship Nineteen disappeared.

The General holstered his gun and turned to Newman: "Now we wait. Meanwhile, you and yours better work out how we can talk to them over there. But first, work out how to push stuff into their space. Just in case, you understand."

Come Tomorrow

The echoes are thunderous, something that keeps away most of the predators down here. This far along, everyone is fatigued. Even the children no longer have bursts of energy. Existence is eating, sleeping and marching to the beat. The chant cadences our footsteps through the netherways: the deep tunnels that were once used to move building materials between the growing United Cities.

"Come tomorrow, we'll live in a far better place."

Each Petacity is a continent-covering sprawl that incorporates everything into an extended conurbation. Intensive automation, overseen by computers fast enough to map DNA in minutes, made them possible. Mankind quickly became dependent on the hyper-infrastructure that provided everything. Then the control systems worked out that growing replacement labour was far more ecologically efficient than building it.

"Come tomorrow, we'll suffer no machine-led pace."

We went from dependent to subservient in two generations. Some objected, of course. But ancient tales of rising against robot masters were glaringly short on overcoming the details. Death came in crush corridors and gas clouds. When you're inside the thing you fight, nobility and righteousness count for little in the immune system versus disease deathmatch.

"Come tomorrow, there will be space for the free man."

Our opponents could dynamically run every possible strategic response for every scenario before we detonated the bomb, landed the second blow, fired the second shot or took the next step. We lost nearly a whole generation in a guerrilla war that more resembled rodents versus pest control than a resistance movement. Finally, cleverer minds prevailed.

"Come tomorrow, we'll do it all with our own hands."

Rats did not fight, they inhabited places man couldn't reach or didn't want. Living underground was not an option and Galifan Scott gave us the answer: United City Seven. The south-polar Petacity had been abandoned as the cold was something that the robots could not overcome without causing ecological harm. They had withdrawn along the netherways, leaving the nascent Petacity to the eternal ice.

"Come tomorrow, the white land will become our home."

The netherways remained, some decrepit, some submerged, all dangerous. But those who survived the first long walks found only a Gigacity core with Petacity foundations unfinished in the face of machine-freezing cold. The founders of Free City One defined the maximum technology that could support millions without processor-based automation. From there they designed a new culture.

"Come tomorrow, our children will be free to roam."

I am a Finder. We go out along the netherways from Free City One, equipped to rescue and retrieve those coming to the end of their long walk. We help the hearty and build cairns for the dead. No more shall we become food or fertiliser depending on our age at dying. The chant gives them hope and strength, keeps them moving toward freedom. It is the last regimen they will have to endure, as Free City One runs on pride, courtesy and idealised British policing.

They say that one day we will reclaim the world. I am one of those who believe that to be a futile objective. We will watch as an alien culture of our ancestors' creation tends the world we so nearly ruined. What the future holds is for our descendants to decide. 'Come tomorrow' is more than the title of a chant to march the freed home.

It is a promise that free humanity will never cease to be.

The Alchemist

The elegant décor did nothing to lift the atmosphere in the room as the small group of officers and dignitaries parted to let Inspector Carbeth through. He strode up to the sprawled body and rapped his cane on the parquet flooring to prompt his man's report.

The detective spoke without looking up from his analyser: "His work, without question."

"What was it this time?"

"A celery stick restructured into tungsten carbide."

Carbeth scowled. The man was making a mockery of his department. Twenty-eight assassinations in nine weeks. The Council was gone. Only His Excellency remained. Drastic measures were required.

A polite cough from the entrance of the room caused all to bow as His Excellency sauntered in.

"My dear Carbeth. This is somewhat of a trial, is it not?"

"Excellency. The man known as the Alchemist is a coward. He slays and then disguises himself as a member of staff, uses his unique molecular manipulation techniques to shape a weapon from a household item, then kills his target without warning or mercy. We are now sure that he remains amongst the staff for the following day and escapes in the evening."

His Excellency looked perturbed: "You mean to say that the Alchemist is amongst the staff here, as we speak?"

Carbeth smiled as a notion became a plan: "Indeed, Excellency. And that is exactly where we want him."

"Really? Do tell."

"Please order the entire staff to assemble in the ballroom. I shall demonstrate."

The ballroom was abuzz with muted conversation as His Excellency, Carbeth and twenty Pacifiers entered. Carbeth received confirmation from the seneschal that all were present.

He drew his flechette pistol and then nodded to the Pacifier Captain: "Kill them all."

The spasmic grunts of unexpected death were drowned out by the crackle of twenty kazers. The silent aftermath was torn by the syncopated hiss of Carbeth's flechette pistol as he shot the seneschal in the back.

"Good god, Carbeth! Are you out of your mind?"

"No, milord. I am killing the Alchemist. For the death of one such as him, the loss of eighty-five serving class is a bargain price."

His Excellency gathered himself.

"Quite exemplary, Carbeth. You might give thought to a Council seat. I find myself in need of men of decisive mien."

His Excellency was less sanguine later, missing his courtesans. Ah well, a couple of bottles of vintage red would tide the night over into the following day and the excitement of getting more staff. He always loved shopping.

Pleasurable anticipation was halted by the sight of a cracker lifting from his caviar, steaming and glowing as it was transformed from foodstuff to molybdenum. As the restructured wafer approached, a dulcet feminine voice spoke from the air to its left.

"It never ceases to amaze me that you are all so fascinated by the technology I use to make my weapons, yet never seek to question the simple ruses I perform to conceal my invisibility."

Granted

I was told that there are many things in this universe you should never take for granted. While several of them are only relevant if you're going to live for a very long time, for the short-lived races I have just found out the hard way that love, trust and guns are at the top of the list.

Susan loved me more than life itself. Being a selfish lowlife, I did things that abused her trust and never really gave them any thought. Today it all came to a head when my trusty pistol failed because I hadn't serviced it in six months despite having several firefights and a couple of drenchings: after all, vintage automatics had a reputation for being utterly reliable.

When Susan threw herself in the way of the projectiles coming for me, I knew that she loved me. Knew that she forgave me. Knew that I would never be able to hold her in my arms, look into her eyes and apologise until I was hoarse.

The beings I had interfered with are Taranti. Amber-skinned bipeds with a bad attitude from birth and a genetic predisposition for life on the criminal side. Famed for being merciless and brutal, they stood around me as I cradled her cooling corpse in my arms. Their leader crouched and lifted my head so he could see into my eyes. I thought he wanted to see the light fade in them after he shot me.

"I see no need to kill you. This penalty of loss is far more than you owe."

With that, he pushed a credstick with a five figure balance into my hand, prying my thumb back from its grip on her shoulder to imprint the ownership pad.

"Drown your inadequacies in drink or drugs. Do something to honour her sacrifice. Either way, our business is complete."

He left me there in the ruined tenement, his henchbeings nodding in agreement with him as they left, muttering between themselves and casting contemptuous glances at me where I knelt in a pool of her blood.

I have added 'opponents' to my list, along with 'tomorrow'. I think that there will have to be more, many more, if I am to commemorate the woman I only realised that I loved as she died to save me.

The Lady Is Not

'The night is yet young', as my grandmother used to say. Apparently it was my grandfather's favourite line before they'd go out to party. She told me about the two of them jetting off to Dubai for breakfast and always being in Shanghai for Chinese New Year. She also bemoaned the difficulty of remaining elegant in the face of a weekend of partying. It was difficult to be elegant on a Sunday evening when you hadn't seen your wardrobe since Friday afternoon.

Fortunately, the times have caught up with the needs of the modern lady. Nanite refresher booths are a feature of every ladies room these days, and my nanofluidic couture allows me to vary my style in response to the slightest need.

Tonight I am a belle dame from the Mississippi Riverboat era, swanning about in a flounced and ruffed creation appearing to be of jade velvet over black leather. My Personal Access Device is transformed into a pair of long lace gloves. Elegance at will.

"Christina, my dear. You look ravishing."

His choice of words makes me smile. Carmody has a reputation for taking the ravishing bit all too seriously. But he knows that I know his tastes. He slides closer with a devastating smile in a face that cost a million. A shame that making his personality pretty is more than cosmetic science can achieve.

"Why don't we take a stroll somewhere quieter, mademoiselle?"

I am just about to tell him to fornicate and depart when my PAD clenches about my wrists as my dress locks up.

Carmody smiles: "Oh dear, cheap bodyware? Wonderful."

My intent to shout for aid is pre-empted by my choker doing just that. Carmody is the very soul of attentiveness, helping me past concerned partygoers, onto the veranda and down into the bowers of the love gardens. The bastard is using a slaver program to turn my couture into a prison. I think about what I'm actually wearing and realise I am, to put it politely, vulnerable to manipulation.

Carmody walks through the starlit evening to a remote nook containing a low table, with me accompanying him like a meal in a serving-droid.

"I think we'll start with obscene and get inventive from there. Any objections? Thought not."

Bastard bastard rapist bastard. I am striving to remain calm when Carmody emits a falsetto shriek and collapses rigidly, his face slamming into the gravel with a satisfying crunch. A figure steps into view as my couture rushes to cover my nakedness.

"My apologies for being a tad late, Miss Christina. Your brother's compliments; he felt that you would object if he insisted that you employed a Safeguard."

Safeguards are personal bodyguards trained, enhanced and equipped with the latest countermeasures for just about anything. Using them is deemed gauche, but after tonight, I'm a convert.

He offers his hand and pulls me up without effort. His impeccable couture changes colour and style to complement mine as I take in his two-metre tall frame. I could become accustomed to this. Turning slightly, I nudge Carmody with my toe.

"What happened to him?"

"I thought it best to dampen his enthusiasm by restricting the volume of his codpiece as I locked his couture. The servants will take him to the gatehouse for collection by the Police ."

I like the edge to his voice as he describes defending me, but I have to confirm my suspicions: "What volume, exactly?"

He actually blushes.

"Four cubic centimetres."

I laugh. My Safeguard and I are going to get along just fine.

I, Rifle

I am a rifle.

There are few like me, but I am unique.

I will fire true.

I will fire straighter than any other.

I know that only hitting the target counts.

I will maintain myself clean and ready.

I will defend my country.

I will master the enemy.

The creed runs through my frontal RAM as it always does, because they think it helps.

"Camera One, pan the crowd."

That is my confirmation. I leave the gathering quietly, entering the stairwell using the card from the security guard I left sleeping in the toilets.

Letting the door close I kill the biomass masquerading as my heart and extend my tibia and humerus, then leap into the gap between the staircases and progress rapidly upward, something only my extended reach permits. Intense security leaves holes. In this case, scanning for life signs in the stairway and movement on the stairs, not dead things moving in the gap between them. Foolishly they considered a metre-wide, sixty storey drop secure.

I slide to the edge of the parapet and reform. My vertebrae alternately revolve ninety degrees to lock, while my head cants back and swings up to locate above where oesophagus-muffler has risen to align with spine-barrel, as lower jaw bifurcates to become the bipod. My left femur rotates and swings back, feeding a 14x110mm tenite forecore TMJ cartridge into the breech that forms my sacral curve, while my arms swing out to stabilise my incline, counterbalanced by my extended right leg.

My Zeiss-lensed eyes feed compensated targeting data to the dedicated math processor that handles all the windage and other variables in less time than it takes Senator Windham's bodyguard to open the door of the limousine.

As his head rises into view, I wait until I see the carotid pulse in his neck in my holographic cross matrix. I exhale death and his head explodes. I use the recoil to slide back, letting my head drop forward as I disengage my osteo-locks and deform. I roll off the parapet and sprint across the roof as alarms start. I dive from the back of the building, sixty storeys up giving me the angle to plunge into the deep end of the public pool across the road and a block down. Water pours from me and startled lovers exclaim, but I am gone over the fence and into the bushes. As I climb the tree by the next road over, the evening run to the recycling plant is passing. I leap from the tree into the back of the truck, amongst metals and electricals that will mask my presence, just as the pool eradicated all detectable miasma of rifle shot. I may have left some pieces of overskin, but it all leads back to the only man who had cloneable cells, like every other piece of vatflesh on the planet.

On the slip road to the industrial estate that surrounds the plant, a rescue and recovery hauler sits. I drop from the back of the recycler and roll under the hauler, pulling myself through the belly hatch into my residence.

William says: "Fine work, Swan."

He means it. He only ever uses my nickname over my designation, S-One, when he's exceptionally pleased. Which means Ruger-Sony are paying him a lot, again.

I settle into a solvent bath and idle my processors. After I'm clean I'll upload the mission log. As I am scoured, I permit my creed to run in private RAM.

I am Sniper One.

I never miss.

Dead Cert

I don't remember what my crime was or who I used to be. I do know that the thought of dying still scares me, which probably explains why I chose Execution Method Three, the one labelled by the media as 'Living Death'. It is actually military service after selective memory erasure. As you're declared dead before you enlist, they can and do push you to the utter limits of what a human is capable of. Seventy percent of penal M3s do not live to graduate.

Whoever I was, I was very smart and must have grown up somewhere interesting. I graduated as CM3, the top half percent of the intake. In animal terms, I have full adult musculature and physical development, which humans rarely achieve. Mentally, I am alert all the time. I could list my statistics and capabilities, but you've seen the vids. Basically I cannot be surprised and am roughly equivalent to twenty men when wreaking havoc.

Right now I am recording this testimony while actively engaged in mayhem. The vid feed you see behind these words is real time, and that is a Kiklamute Marine I have just thrown one-handed through the brick wall shielding his comrades over there. I can do this for three days before needing rest. Two days without water. One day with what would usually be called a fatal injury.

M3s are the pinnacle of human development, while CM3s are quite possibly the deadliest human warriors to ever exist. We have become a warrior elite. It has been decided that restricting this elite to criminals is unfair on the many who undoubtedly could contribute. This is why I'm on every channel tonight. A Kiklamute effective is far deadlier than a normal human effective. We are losing this war of attrition despite having better tactics and starting out with superior numbers.

Do you feel that you're capable of, or destined for, more? Then volunteer for the first draft of the Invincibles Cadre. You'll be taught by the best, including me. When you finish training, you'll be one of the first M3Vs or possibly a CM3V commanding a team of M3s. As we all saw at Detrencha, that sort of force can change the tide of battle.

Do you want to make a difference? Then download the selection pack and I'll see you soon.

The broadcast switches to prerecorded blurb and my monitor indicator goes out. Time to get proper messy; I leap a small house and descend on the Kiklamute fire team that had been trying so hard to ruin my presentation. I don't even draw on them, going in unarmed. Two minutes later I'm surrounded by corpses and smeared in a decent quantity of orange gore at last.

"They're retreating!"

"Too right. We've chopped the odds down to under twenty to one and Squad Eight has just rolled in."

That brought our strength up to eighty M3 and four CM3 with me at the top as longest serving. The Kiklamute were down to under fifteen hundred effectives, even if you included the crews of their mechanised division. This was going to be a massacre and they knew it. We always joked that Kiklamute Marines only qualified so they could get the power suits that let them run away even quicker.

After a circular gesture of my hand over my head, I point toward the enemy. Even a judge could not pronounce such a final sentence of death. My M3s go in fast and silent. It scares the Kiklamute silly that we make no noise. It's only the après-slaughter party that can get a little raucous.

"Good broadcast, Tommo. The selection pack has been grabbed over two hundred thousand times since you announced it. Early infosnooping indicates the Kiklamute are mortified about us openly recruiting more Living Dead. "

"Thank you, Governor. If you'll excuse me, I have another victory to orchestrate."

"Good man. I'll let you get stuck in."

I need to ensure we stick to the strategic plan, the one that ensures we never hit the Kiklamute as fast or as hard as we can. Because I *do* still fear death, and I know damn well that when this war ends, they'll kill every last M3, no matter what letters come before or after that designation.

Daughter of Eons

Between the interstices of creation something slips at a speed beyond reckoning. It is answering a call so distant that even the whispering of the void between stars is a cacophony in comparison, yet possessed of an attraction so primal that not even a black hole could divert it: blood shall ever be stronger than duty.

There was a legend in my homeland that persisted despite all the science that the people from the stars brought to my world. It tells of a god, long ago, who having created the heavens and all the stars and worlds that fill them, decided that our world, the last he made and thus the finest, needed something to mark it as the pinnacle of his endeavours.

He pondered for a long time. Stars died and empires faded. Still he pondered. Then, upon seeing the grace of a girl child on our world in the face of the suffering inflicted upon her family in the wake of a war, he decided.

Why war on this most perfect of his worlds? Because civilisations need war to grow, just like forests need to burn to the ground to be renewed.

Thus the girl child vanished from the peak of a mountain where she cried for her people and the Quinexoryn came into being in a flash of creation that stroked the heavens with violet lightning. She became his gift to man: a creature of immeasurable power, utter compassion, near-invulnerability and incredible longevity. The legend continues, telling us that after the passage of many centuries, the daughter of a stoneworker was transformed into the next Quinexoryn and her father laid the circle of slabs that crown the peak to this day. The mother of the third Quinexoryn carved the four great uprights that mark the compass points about that circle.

So it has gone and so it has been, from times of legend, through great wars, natural disasters and the coming of the star men, a constant of our world that brings the curious and the god-seeking from across the galaxy to stand upon that circle of stone, chanting their litanies and uttering their hopes. But the Quinexoryn is away doing her lord's work. The legend says that she visits any world that the god set man upon, should they need her: dwelling there for a while, an ineluctable presence of mercy incarnate.

I shuffle up to the gate and Bertin son of Lubrech steps out to greet me, his off-world clothes garish in the soft light of the moon. In the gatehouse, a screen plays some entertainment, or news, or maybe both. My old eyes and mind cannot cope with that rush of information. I prefer to read slowly and savour every word.

"Moon shine fair upon you, Elder Sarnosian. You go to keep vigil?"

"May your fortunes rise as inevitably as the sun, Bertin. I do indeed. My last vigil, for I fear I shall not see another summer."

Bertin nods, his youth making him uncomfortable in the face of such a matter-of-fact acceptance of death.

"Go you safe, Elder. I shall be here with tea and fresh bread upon your descent."

"You are a good man, Bertin. I look forward to breaking my fast with you on the morrow."

He opens the gate and I hobble through, gritting my teeth and setting my eyes upon the single upright visible high above. It will be a trial, tonight's climb. Behind me, I hear the door to the gatepost close, cutting off the foreign media, the night relaxing as the intrusive presence is stifled.

The moon has fully risen by the time I reach the top and I permit myself to collapse into gasping repose against the southern upright. This place and I have known each other too long for it to regard my sitting as any lack of respect.

I lean my head back against the upright, the cool stone leaching away the sweat upon my bald crown. For ninety-three years I have made this climb, on the occasion of the last moon of each spring. Ninety-four years ago I only watched from the gate as my Pasmina made her way up to this place, torn between wishing and dread as she disappeared from view. I thought she would return, until the skies were riven by mauve lightning as the moon set. A new Quinexoryn had risen and, despite my joy, the father in me wept. She would traverse the heavens, seeing things beyond my ken, working peace upon worlds like I made tribesmen see sense.

Even though my daughter was gone, I knew she would live far beyond my lifespan, ensuring man continued to grow. It had taken me a very long time to understand that beyond a certain size, a civilisation is not like a forest. If it burns in the fires of war, nothing good will rise from the ashes. At that point, a new balance has to be applied. From my discussions with the elders of the star men who visited me, the Quinexoryn was the arbitrator of that balance. My daughter had become something that was regarded as divinity itself on some of the worlds she had intervened upon.

This merging of science, religion and myth had been the renaissance of my world. Because so many came to study the place of the Quinexoryn's creation, they settled here. Because so many of the star men's respected elders had settled here, the star men made this world their place of learning. They named my world Alexandria, as they just could not pronounce our name for it correctly without palate surgery; our ancient 'high tongue' being a challenge even for my people and falling into disuse because of that.

In my waning decade I realised that the Quinexoryn had intervened upon her homeworld. We were insignificant in the greater schemes of the galaxy and our cultures had been slowly fading. Now our world was vibrantly alive, populated by the learned and the wise from every world. But they needed to converse and in some happenstance of fashion and practicality, adopted our 'low tongue' as the language to enable that. Our culture has been studied in depth and even the high tongue has been proposed for a revivification by one of the avian races that found it easy to pronounce and appealingly arcane.

I wondered, on this night of all nights, if she knew what she had done? Had her creation itself been her first intervention? This spoke of a higher power so forcefully that several major religions now had tribes of students here dedicated to researching that one instance and its implications.

I take out my flask and have a sip of karkade, a tea from a world far away, made from the blooms of a plant called hibiscus that has adapted well to our lowlands. Its biggest advantage is to be refreshing whether served hot or cold and because of that it has swiftly become a traveller's staple.

The moon is high and peeks occasionally from behind the great clouds that promise a blustery day tomorrow, where driven dust will send all but the most determinedly curious to seek shelter. The circle of stone is cool beneath my legs as I reluctantly admit once again why I keep this vigil. It is not an 'ancient custom' or 'priestly ritual'; it is a father wondering if his daughter is all right. For all her apparent power and success, is she happy? How silly that thought seems in the face of what she became and will be for long after I am dust. But every year I come up here on the anniversary of the night that she disappeared and concede that I am nought but a father, and I worry about my little girl.

There is a flash of light like when the engines exploded in a ship at the spaceport, except that this explosion is accompanied by utter silence.

She is here.

The sparkling energy of her wing membranes sinks back into the shaped roil of star-flux and lightning that comprises the bones of her wings, the crown upon her head and the very clothing she wears upon her translucent form. But her face is not translucent. A woman of timeless beauty stares at me with eyes I know so well, for all that they are older. The innocence of a child and the strength of a woman who has seen sorrow and decided for the best many times, combined in a gaze that sees all that this place is.

My daughter, a goddess. I see now why she is worshipped. Such implicit power carried with such calm, gentle grace. There is no coercion in her, no threat. She is mercy given form to ensure that mercy is given.

I cannot speak. I hope she knows what I think, of my love and my concern, because she will not be able to see it in my eyes through the tears of wonder and joy that fill them and spill down my face.

She gives a little smile and her head dips. I see her lips move, but the words do not arrive until her face is once more serene and unmoving.

"I am fine, Papa."

I am blinded by a greater flash than that of her arrival and when it fades, I am alone again. I look up at the stars and laugh until my tears dry.

Has there ever been a father more proud? I doubt it.

Reunion Blues

Sandrava's plans are in ruins. His people are either arrested, dead or futilely resisting arrest. His formerly-hidden headquarters burns brightly below me. He stands behind me, a shock pistol pointed at my head. At this range, my brains will be jelly before I hit the ground.

"Nineteen years! Damn your eyes, Herech! I put everything into this."

His voice trails off in bafflement. Far below, tiny figures run about. They can't get up here in time to save me.

"Why, Herech? Why?"

I turn to face him, his goatee stark against his pallor, his eyes too bright in the moonlight.

"Because you covered every other option. Every agency that could help to stop you answered to your Union. I couldn't reach the authorities because of members in every key post."

His brow furrows: "Exactly. We were ready."

I smile ruefully at him: "You were wrong. You sent me in to spy on them and all I found was truth."

"Truth?"

"The Fairmen. They're not aliens; they were created to rule by our ancestors. To stop us warring for power by being the holders of the power. To let mankind achieve by removing its main detractor."

His face flushes and zealotry widens in his eyes, yet I see fear behind it: "They told you the truth and you couldn't handle it."

His eyes narrow as he prepares a stock rebuttal; his lies will not give easily, despite being worn from overuse. I cut those dead too: "No, I did not succumb, because there was nothing to succumb to. All they had was evidence and common sense."

I point down at the ruins and out over the city where firefights still rage.

"The only source of destruction on this planet is you. You're not fighting for freedom. You're fighting for the power they hold because you need vindication. Altruism be damned. You want to be king and you're prepared to ruin this world to have your reign."

His lips part to show his teeth, but it's not a smile.

"Damn you. I would have been better than them. Humans would be nobility."

"What use is nobility? Something to offer as a reward? To make people fight over privilege: that's feudal."

I see the gleam in his eyes. He wants it all back: nations, factions, everybody fighting just to hold their own. With him looking down, choosing who rises and who falls.

"It's over. I gave her everyone. Every corrupted official, every gunman. There will be no resurgence and no martyrs."

He stares me hard in the face and finally understands. His voice is tremulous: "Mathilde?"

I let him have it: "It seems your aversion to Fairmen became a cause right after you discovered a taste for your so-called aliens."

He recoils like I've become radioactive, eyes widening as realisation gathers suppressed truths and slams the whole mess into his battered psyche. With a wordless cry of denial, he presses the pistol under his jaw and pulls the trigger.

She had been right: Confronting him with irrefutable evidence of his 'xeniality' would be too much for his delusions to bear.

I step over the body of the man who shaped ten years of my life before I discovered he was my father. I hadn’t known when he sent me to spy on the Fairmen because I could pass as one. I found out that I could pass as one because my mother was one of them, the supposedly alien rulers he reviled.

Fairman Mathilde, my mother, is waiting at my new home to introduce me to a family I never knew I had.

Suriel

The problem with early FTL journeys was the failure rate. Just like the first elevators, the disappearances were hidden from the public to prevent rejection of the innovation. It was the mid twenty-second century before better understanding and implementation reduced the errors to less than one in a hundred thousand.

Back in the early twenty-first century, there was an audio-visual series that had dinosaurs appearing through time portals. A scientist in the twenty-second century named Eduard Samson was a fan of that series. An intuitive leap led him to postulate that the FTL disappearances were due to the vessels vanishing through time. Now those time-lost on their outbound journeys are probably not an issue beyond the tragedy of their loss. However, those time-lost on their return could have appeared in Earth's past. Backtracking was a brilliant concept that he documented with flair and diligence. His treatise gained him some awards and was then forgotten.

Three centuries later, Samson's treatise resurfaced when our second generation temporal mapping revealed the backtracks: our term for stress fractures in time itself, that we knew through bitter experience could escalate into reversion zones, where entire swathes of history disappear. It's terrifying to watch every record of an event morph into something else and know that by tomorrow, your own memory will have made the same adjustment.

That's why the Temporal Rectification Taskforce was formed. We're a small group, because the psychological impact of what we do takes a rather peculiar outlook. Our job is to repair the backtracks. The complication is finding out where they exited and what impact they had, if any. Then we have to deal with any untoward influence they may have had on whatever time period they arrived in and we have to do it in a way that fits with recorded history, including mythology.

Rescue is impossible as an FTL infrastructure does not exist, let alone something that can support Temporal Loop Transit, and size limitations on self-contained units preclude anything bigger than a one-man vessel.

Take a look at history. The number of anomalous beings and civilisations that end catastrophically occurs so often it is regarded as the ancient archivist's standard trite explanation. Eduard Samson's treatise weighed the odds and stated that the actions of a future agency to correct backtrack impacts would have to be treated and reported as supernatural action by the observers of the time.

After the first few attempts at interactive intervention, we had to adopt a no-contact approach. When the time-stranded find out that you've only come to ensure they meet their end in the historically correct manner, they always become hostile.

So we do our research, determine the best corrective action and apply it regardless of the usual moral considerations. In fact, regardless of any moral considerations. Our only measure of success is a backtrack fading from the maps, indicating a successful mitigation.

I was the first member of the action team. I take the horror mitigations, the apocalypses. The stuff that makes formerly dedicated people hesitate or resign, suddenly doubting the validity of our purpose due to the scale of annihilation needed.

My ship is ready, carrying a payload that even made the ordnance loading crews blanch. No one knows if the warheads will cope with a time journey. If I survive this trip, I will finally deserve the name that our research team have determined is historically the one most likely to have been applied to TRT agents performing mitigations.

Tonight I go to sink Atlantis.

In the Pink

Duncan looked at me with a smile and said: "This should be interesting."

Interesting? We're stuck in a tiny all-terrain rover as a wall of pink vapour eight metres high churns after us at a speed marginally faster than our top-end on this terrain.

Why did I agree to going on an expedition with the man I'm divorcing? The chance of seeing an Eflubian spawnworld, a planet dedicated to the mating rituals of the greatest species of sentient ooze to ever exist. After the shooting war stopped, they had proven to be disturbingly like us in many ways. Within a decade of that, holidaying on the other race's homeworld was the top luxury travel destination.

So when we were offered the opportunity to visit one of the previously unseen spawnworlds, the few posts available were prized billets. Duncan and I had been separated for a couple of years, but as we had both worked at the top of the same fields before transferring to the new science of xenobiology, it was unfortunately inevitable we would meet again.

Flabia was an interesting planet with minimal vegetation and vast seas, a planet far older than Earth, yet from the same class: another lure to those who wanted to see what Earth would be like a few thousand years down the line.

So we arrived and were given some very odd instructions. When reduced to the basics, they meant we could go anywhere we liked unless an Eflubian asked us not to, and if we saw a pink cloud rolling along the ground, we should run away from it.

Two months later we had enough information to keep us in grants and publishing deals for several lifetimes. I found that working alongside Duncan was not a strain. We knew each other's ways in the field, there was no friction, no awkward moments. So on the day before we were due to leave, when Duncan asked me to go with him out onto the great salt plains to retrieve the last sensor array, I agreed.

After collecting the array, we were a quarter of the way back when I saw a huge pink cloud rolling up behind us. Within a few minutes, we knew that avoiding it was impossible. After placing a distress call to base, we pulled over and buckled in for a storm of unknown violence. Anything that the Eflubians advised us to avoid was sure to be unpleasant.

The cloud enveloped the rover and we heard the frame groan. This wasn't just a cloud! The compression sprung some panels and both of us unbuckled and frantically reached about, stuffing cloth or anything into the splits where a pink mist spurted in. Duncan took his shirt off and I was down to my underwear when we both realised that the rover was filled with this pink mist. As we stared at each other in horror, I was doubled up by a wave of burning nausea that suddenly crystallised into something more as the world spun and I blacked out.

I came round draped over the back of the driver's seat. The agony of even the slightest movement made me pass out. The second time I came round, I had fallen into the passenger seat. I looked down and saw a foot resting on the centre console. Leaning round despite the pain, my gaze followed the limb until I beheld Duncan, lying naked with an expression of agony frozen on his dead features. At that, I passed out again.

That was how the rescue crews found me, stark naked and curled in a foetal position in the passenger seat of the rover. Over the following week, the Eflubians reluctantly filled in the gaps that the investigation team did not have the understanding to answer.

The pink clouds were not clouds. They were massive gatherings of Eflubians engaged in reproduction. A roiling orgy of protoplasmic lust that secreted pheromones that the Eflubians had suspected might be able to influence humans. Duncan and I had proved that. Immersed in a miasma of Eflubian sex hormones, we had frenziedly fucked each other until something gave. According to forensics, Duncan's death had not actually stopped me, I had continued until I collapsed from exhaustion. The only thing that saved me was the multi-orgasmic capability of women.

I returned to Earth and underwent counselling for a year. I'm recovered now, even have a new boyfriend. But he has learned that raspberry yoghurt or similar will either reduce me to hysterical tears or make me so horny I will literally tear his clothes off. He adjusted well: for our first anniversary, he filled our bath with pink custard.

I hospitalised him.

Jewels and Blood

The drill slides sideways like it's got a mind of its own, so I straighten up to lift it clear of the crystal. My vision blurs and I pause to gauge which of the two reasons applies. With a bark of laughter I realise it's the good option: too much rum.

"Hey Andy, you slackin' again?"

Milt's unbelievable, able to track the world around him like a sober person.

"Not enough blood in my alcohol system, ya fruit. I'm declarin' snacktime. You in?"

"Goddam, boy. You goin' nine-oh-one on me?"

That's the medical code for saturation, when your body cannot metabolise enough alcohol to keep the Fenden at bay and let you work.

"Not a chance. I did half a bottle too soon is all."

"That's the problem with Jamaican. You should switch to Russian."

"It's got no flavour, Milt. If I'm going to pickle my ass, I've gotta have somethin' I can savour."

"You always did read too much and drink too fancy for a jeweller."

"Bugger off. I've got cold hog and fresh kiwis; last chance."

"I never said anythin' bad about your goo-er-may eatin' habits, boy. I'll be there afore you have canvas up."

I grin as I turn and use the drill to punch a post-hole in black rock. Sure enough, I'm just swinging the awning up onto the pole when Milt appears and grabs the far side. In a few moments we're cross-legged in the shade savouring meat and fruit. From where we are, you can see the company enclave on the horizon. Between us and them lies the glittering expanse of the lowlands, shining like the treasure it conceals. Randell is a pretty planet, the vast crystalline plains reflecting whatever light is about, day or night. Under the plains in striated crystalline clumps is the wealth of the universe, the purest of which make any optical device better and the least of which make women feel appreciated.

When the company opened up the digs, they franchised the 'jewellers' and supplied the drugs that make our bodies inedible to the Fenden, the translucent gas things who just love drinking a human for dinner. Bloodmist outbreaks were a problem initially; when Fenden gorge and get amped up on warm human fluids, they group together and go into a slaughter frenzy. Made mining almost impossible until some doctor discovered that certain chemical additives make humans taste bad. The company had us jewellers over a barrel until Marty Grufe discovered that being pissed up was just as effective. You could buy two months supply of spirits for the price of a one-week shot of the company's patent protector. Pretty soon, the only sober people on Randell lived in the company enclave. If you're outside these days, you're either drunk or dead.

Milt slaps my shoulder and points. In the middle distance, a ruby cloud whirls by. I wonder who we lost today. It's so easy to get so engrossed in a rich lode of gems that you let your regular swigging go. Do that for a couple of hours and you get to be edible, which is always fatal. Every jeweller has a few Fenden nearby, just waiting for him to get careless. That's why smart jewellers pair up: to live long enough to enjoy their earnings.

I lift a bottle of rum and raise it to Milt. He lifts his vodka bottle and clinks it against mine.

"Here's to the gems an' the booze never runnin' out."

"Damn straight. Sláinte!"

Tariff

The Neosatian hits me at the base of my spine so hard that I flip over backwards and land heavily, knocking the wind from me. By the time I get my breath, I cannot move because it's sitting on me, front paws on my shoulders.

I stare up into the trio of glowing green eyes while slowly sliding my hand toward the shock-rod at my belt. Its burgundy-tipped ears cant forward and it shakes its head in negation. I stop moving.

"Damo Adraste. You are under arrest for sentient slaughter in the thousand-being range. You are also charged with fleeing penalty, your fugitive run of eight years removing all appeal options for both charges. Although it will be duly noted as the longest evasion on record."

The owner of the dulcet voice strolls up, still beautiful in the bodysuit that leaves nothing to the imagination, whilst simultaneously scaring you out of any interest beyond survival. She settles down by me, resting against the alley wall after relieving me of the rod. She catches my gaze and smiles.

"It was always going to end like this. Did you really believe the bollox about Neosatians being avoidable?"

I had hoped it was true. The Mondocalm had gifted humanity with twenty of these enhanced creatures, saying they were all we would need to usher in a new era of crimelessness. The huge black lupines were immediately labelled ‘godwolves’ by the media.

“This furry gentleman is Ebenezer. He’s very pleased to finally meet you.”

The jaws part to reveal a lot more teeth than I am comfortable with at this range.

“While we wait for the custody patrol, Ebenezer wants me to tell you why you could not escape.”

I look up at the godwolf. I would swear that the damn thing is grinning at me.

“Imagine that every living thing leaves a trail. Think of them as multicoloured lines drawn through time and space, with every one being unique. Normal dogs can do amazing things with scent alone. The Mondocalm took the lupine variant of that ability and mated it with their ability to perceive sentient contrails in a four dimensional continuum. Ebenezer and his kin can never lose your trail as long as you exist.”

Well, that explained a lot. From the deep mines on Spira to the skytowns of Ruben, from the asteroid fields of Cantor to the spiral wastelands of the Eternal Reaches, Pursuit Marshal Sheba Griffon and her loyal godwolf had kept on reappearing, no matter what I did. The fact that the rest of humankind treated the godwolves with an almost religious awe meant I could never get any support for trying old fashioned methods of losing pursuers permanently. Sure, I had blown up several places, but bombs are so damn inaccurate.

“Why exactly does he want me to know?”

“So you can tell all your fellow inmates. Eventually you felons will realise that getting away with it is not even an outside option.”

I had done it. Five years and the tariff for my original crime went from mortal to custodial.

"So I'm going to jail?"

"I think there will be several jails between here and Earth."

And a free trip home. I smile.

"Then you're going to be incinerated. Tariff reduction is waived as crimes during flight are deemed contiguous with the original felony."

Damn.

Old Ways

They left me. I was screaming into the mike and they took off anyway. I rounded that last corner in time to see the tail lights of the chopper disappearing over Sherwood. I still remember Benny's last words in my headset: "Skipper says we gotta go, buddy. He's not risking the squad and the helo for one mutt, he says. Good luck, mate."

Bloody typical. Everyone has their moment to shine, to rise above their past and do right. Captain Skander decided to take an opportunity instead. They had time to evac me, but his lily-livered outlook needed a bigger margin. A shit-scared commander is useful to nobody. Especially the useful nobody who's bucking for his job.

I look down from the tower to see a group of ferals fighting over a female, who's giving as good as she gets by the look of it. Tatters of clothing flying in the fading light and their snarls indispersed with part-words. The losers will be tonight's meal.

The virus was christened 'High-Nine' by the media and came out of Rio de Janiero by all accounts. It's not a zombie epidemic or a liquefy-your-guts horror. The massive fever kills many, but those who survive are mindless. Every trace of the higher cognitive functions, which are the only thing separating man from the apes, is lost. What remains is a two-legged animal that serves only its basic needs: food, shelter and reproduction. They can't open anything that cannot be torn apart by fingers and nails, so the tinned wealth of the world lies unused amidst hordes of starving cannibal hunter-gatherers, along with ammunition, medical supplies and all the useful stuff us survivors need.

After being abandoned, I spent several days in a daze, just running and reacting - with more time than I like to admit curled in a ball in out of the way boltholes. Then my ammo ran out and my rations went too. It was a chilly early morning under a gibbous moon when this Welsh laddie decided to live, not just exist. I had the training, I had the discipline. All I needed was the will, and that came before the moon set.

I think it's about a year later: exact timekeeping being a casualty of my discarding all unnecessary things. As the ferals drifted out of the cities in search of fodder, I chose to make my base in the centre of one. Nottingham Council House lent itself nicely to a one-squaddie lair at the heart of a fortified and booby-trapped building. Then I found Charlie and his crew, which led to a leadership contest that left Mick and Gloria with me. The rest of them tried to take Council House off us twice. The third attempt attracted the attention of a pack of passing ferals and those who survived that either fled or succumbed to High-Nine. A week after that people started turning up at the door. The noise had attracted them. As the Council House is huge, I let them in. Of course, over the following weeks factions arose. The confrontations from that resulted in the larger part of the group heading off for the Nottingham Business School, led by a charming executive type called Chris. I have dim opinions of where that is going to end up. The one advantage is that I kept every one of the military or ex-military types and most of the independent thinkers. In the modern forces, you can't be an idiot and you cannot help but see the realities of the world. Makes for a tight group of thirty-eight. We've got planters and even a lawn on the roof and the greenhouse is built. We've emptied every shop within a couple of miles and skirmished with the lot from the Business School, but they're crap fighters and worse tacticians. The Council House is fortified to the nines and I reckon it'll take armour to get in if we don't want them in.

The great thing about my mob is the determination not to languish and just survive. We've got the beginnings of communications and a lot more guns than you'd think for a British city, plus a huge library that gets a lot of use. From listening in on the radio, it seems that some parts of the world survive largely untouched, but they don't want refugees to strain their resources and some of the landlocked borders are pretty grim.

We reckoned on staying put for as long as possible. Life was good, even if we would have had to take the Business School in the spring. The competition for resources would have become critical and as they were not open to negotiating with us 'knuckleheads', the only option was force and unlike them, we know how and when to apply it.

A few months back, my headset clicked for channel change one night. So after doubling the guards, muting any traces of 'advanced' survival and getting everybody ready for a ruck, I switched and clicked back.

"Bloody hell, Reynolds. You still going?"

"I'm going good, Benny. How's you?"

"The Captain bought it and we're down on supplies, so someone had the bright idea of scavenging the towns again. As we were in range, I had to try."

"Good lad. I'm over at the Business School, hidden from the survivor group there and living on the fringes of their op. Being civvies, it's a bit crap but it's my only chance as the bunch around the Council House got infected a few weeks back. At least this lot scavenged the place to the walls before the ferals took over. Look, the headset's about to die, so see you lot soon?"

"Sure will, buddy."

I tore off the headset and dropped it into my half pint of Guinness. Then I sent everyone to the basement shelter except my motley squad, who tooled up and headed for the roof with me.

From there we watched the Business School mob fail to stop anything, then watched the Chinooks descend when the gunfire became sporadic. They looted the place hard as I suspected they would, before heading off into the night, back to wherever they had come from. The demolition charges were a bit over the top, but it told me a lot about what my old unit had become a part of. It was simple intelligence gathering, seeing if I was still about. Fortunately I had considered that during my days as a lone survivor, about gathering intel to get back in with the squad when they passed by again. When I acquired my own group, the thinking got darker and I'm damn glad that it did.

Since that night, we've established caches of supplies across the city, all with anti-tampering traps of the total destruction variety. A lot of the abandoned vehicles about town have been transformed into solid barricades while remaining outwardly just wreckage. Plus one of the survivors from the Business School is a builder. Several buildings have been rigged to fall as well, thanks to his knowledge of architecture and of where the construction companies kept their demolition charges. We're weak against anything that flies, but some of the crazy inventors have scavenged together some wickedly powerful ballistae that are set up in hides on the tall buildings. We do what we can. I never knew napalm was so easy to make, either. University professors are handy people to have about.

I'm expecting a battle one day. I hope it'll never come and we can continue to transform Nottingham Centre into a proper survivor community, possibly with negotiated agreements with other uninfected groups. But I'd be an idiot to not prepare for a confrontation. Ferals we can deal with easily now, not even killing them. They're just a dangerous animal to be contained and kept away from us.

Depressingly, it's the end of the world as we knew it and I'm still having to waste precious time preparing to defend myself against other humans.

The View From Here

After the successes of breeding for telepaths and telekinetics, they moved on to the more esoteric strains. My mum and dad had the right genetic markers for the rarest of them: precognition. So they joined the program and had two kids with everything paid for.

I was the first, "a beautiful baby boy who turned into a reclusive weirdo", according to grandma. My sister, Sandy, was even better looking and far better at being social.

Precogs have affinities. Attunement to earthquakes, fire, weather, aircraft and anything else you can imagine. The range is forever expanding.

Sandy is lying motionless on the bed in intensive care, the scars of her multiple suicide attempts a roadmap of sadness on her forearm. This time she stole a shotgun. The fact she is alive is purely down to the fact that the gun was too big for her to hold properly against anywhere vital. She's lost an arm and one side of her face is a ruin, but she's alive.

"Hey Stu."

Her voice is a whisper, but my lil' sis is back.

"I screwed up, didn't I?"

I smile through the tears. “Yeah, sis. You missed. But I’m well happy you did.”

She reaches slowly and I take her hand. She squeezes it as hard as she can, which isn’t very hard at all.

“Why, sis? You were there. Fully manifested at rank six. That six-year view means you’re set for life.”

A tear rolls down her cheek.

“My affinity, Stu. It’s disease. All I see is families dying horribly, all the time. My six-year view means I see them all, starting with whatever causes the most pain and death.”

That’s common. Seems that the more people in agony, the stronger the ‘signal’ to be picked up.

“If only you could manifest, Stu. At least I could share.”

Oh sis, I’m so sorry. I never realised that my secret would cause you to feel so alone.

“Sis, you’ve got to promise to keep a crazy secret before I tell you something.”

Her one eyebrow raises and she nods, then winces in pain.

“I manifested when I was eight. At rank fifty-five.”

Her eye widens and she nearly crushes my hand.

“Why didn’t you tell anyone? That’s forty ranks beyond the best. What’s your affinity?”

I smile and lean closer.

“I’m only telling you because you have to know you’re never alone. I’m always going to be here for you.”

“But what’s your affinity?”

“Me.”

She looks puzzled. “What?”

"My affinity is me. Nothing more. I know when every member of the family dies, because I have felt my grief. But I don't know which family member it is. I do know that I will outlive all of you."

She smiles. "So that's how you got here so quick. You precog'd your pain over my shotgun surgery."

I nod. "Too right, little sister. Don't you ever try that again…"

Her eyes widen as I drop into farsee without warning. Then I'm back and smiling even wider: "Good girl. Some events I felt have gone."

She squeezes my hand: "Rank fifty-five? Why there, do you think?"

I look at her, a sorrowful smile spreading across my face.

"That's when I die, sis."

"That's amazing. Why don't you announce?"

"I really don't think that knowing the exact time I will be taking a shit for the next forty-four years is going to help the world."

She laughs so hard that the automed sedates her. I stay, holding her hand and knowing that my little sister is going to make it through.

Counterinsurgent

I've never seen a gun this big. Not a pistol, anyway. I can put my fist into the barrel without touching the sides. There's a lot of complicated stuff wrapped around it, but it's basically a huge single-shot. The cartridge is dull grey with a brass base. I weigh it in my hand and look across the table at Joel.

"This is not subtle."

He is emotionless: "It is the only way."

"After all the research, the only option is to shoot the ambassador?"

"It makes a statement. For all his race's superiority, they are still vulnerable to a human."

"How about my entry with this monstrosity?"

"This gun's twin is in the base of the replica of the Statue of Liberty in the lobby. It's loaded but the trigger spacer is in place and the safety is on. Your invitation to the event will give you all the access you need. Remember, you need to pull the trigger as he's leaving."

I nod understanding and take my leave as soon as I can politely do so, their best wishes ringing hollow to my ears.

The Haerkoon look like turquoise descendants of the dinosaur dilophosaurus and many old films depict similar neotherapoda hunting and killing humans. The fact that the Haerkoon are fish-eating philosophers who consider Earth's oceans to be the greatest wonder in two hundred worlds is ignored by those wishing to spread fear and hatred.

The following night I add a small note to my ensemble and make my way to the venue. At the second checkpoint I see my deliverance.

"Keracki! Do I have to go through this?"

She pushes her cap back and widens her eyes in mock innocence.

"You could be Earth Lib, with a load of bioweapons up your ass."

I shake my finger at her: "Bad minx. Now come over here and clear me."

Jade relents and lets me through. As she gives me a hug, I slip the note into her waistband. Her eyes track to mine and she blinks acknowledgement.

The congress is a success and the gala, introduced by Prime Minister Adelmann and Ambassador Sadiquan themselves, is a marvel. The finale, which combines Noh with Haerkoon Honour Rituals and presents it in a gravity suppression field, is awesome beyond words.

I make sure that I'm the first to enter the lobby, but Jade and her squad have already secured it. A careful scout about finds the missing piece. The replica Statue of Liberty hides more than the big pistol. There's an unconscious Haerkoon in there too. Jade just stares at me with her finest 'explain or die' expression. I make her wait until the dignitaries have departed.

"He said 'pull the trigger', not 'shoot him'. Former Major Joel Johnstone is not a man known for ambiguity in his orders. They needed me to pull the trigger, and to do so in the lobby of the Grande Splendir Hotel as the delegates were leaving. Hitting anyone was irrelevant. The explosion of the exotic combustible in the shell, along with a dead Haerkoon and my body, would have allowed Joel to start a campaign to ruin the peace so many have worked so hard for."

The main doors swing open and the rest of my strike team enter.

Haphrin smiles and salutes: "We got eighteen of them, sir. No Johnstone."

"Very well. Holo their memories and let the MI27 computers handle the correlation."

I look down at my rumpled suit.

"I'll be in combats and ready to roll in an hour. Until then, get fed and sorted. Because after that, we're not stopping until Earth Lib is finished."

ICU

I'm wandering down a back alley in Bognor at three in the morning, bucket and brush in hand, when a comms click lets me know that one of the locals is near.

"Oi. What you doin'?"

I raise my tools and turn to face him.

"Touchin' up the treatments. Easier to see the gaps by moonlight."

He's a skinny lad with his cap on sideways, can of beer in one hand and an unlit joint in the other. In Cairo he'd have a coffee instead of a beer. In Rio, an automatic instead of the smoke, because the smoke would be hanging from the corner of his mouth.

"We see him, Tim. Knockdown time?"

That's my cover team; no idea where they are but I always know they've got my back.

"Hold on that."

Skinny and dim looks confused.

"What did you say?"

I smile and lower my bucket arm.

"Said the damn bucket's heavy. Now, can I go finish what I'm doing?"

"Yeah, yeah mate. No problem. The treatments really sorted the fungus and shit around here, so you're welcome. Mind if I tag along?"

"Not at all."

The cover team heckles me mercilessly as I wander around, seeing nonexistent gaps to apply my 'patching' on, while my new best friend Jimmy witters on about racin' zak, skimmers and suebins. By context I'm sure one of those is music and one of them is either female or redoll, but don't ask me to pick which one.

Two hours later and I'm done. I say goodbye to Jimmy, accept a swig from his can and casually walk off down the road. Turning the corner I jog back to the truck, clip the brush inside the bucket and seal both in their canister.

Skippy and Mika are up front and we're rolling before I finish closing the door. Mika is shivering. Gentry by blood, she gets twitchy around lower class areas, like its contagious or something. A beep calls me to switch channels.

"Tim, I take it we're done?"

"Confirmed. All the eyes are on clear fields."

"Will your new friend remember?"

"Negative. I dropped a membomb in his beer when I had a swig."

"Tidy. I like that. Hold a moment… Confirm we have full coverage. Good work. Go offline for twelve."

I switch channel to the cover team and call them off, then lean forward and grin.

"It's a proper job and we've got twelve hours free."

The banter that starts there tails off into silence on the long drive to Salisbury. I stretch out in the back and spend a while peeling little bits of seepoxy off my fingers and boots. It's incredible stuff, thousands of simple cameras in a transparent epoxy. The cameras were used decades ago for battlefield surveillance, scattered as a cloud and just abandoned when their tiny charge ran out. Then came conductive lacquers and the combination is giving us surveillance everywhere. The lacquer has a side effect of damp retardation and mold prevention. A great excuse to cover urban areas in the stuff. All you have to do then is dab some seepoxy up on the best viewpoints, install receivers in local traffic towers, piggyback on their spare bandwidth and presto! Total overlook and no-one knows.

Criminals and subversives are beside themselves trying to find out how they're getting caught. Its worthy work and my team are good at it. But we've been working on specific cloaking devices in our downtime. Because we of all people know that those at the top might go a little too far with this.

Proof

There is a philosophical concept that states we are nothing but the distillations of our mistakes. I do believe that makes me over a hundred proof.

“Ser Partha, please come down.”

The spire is atop the tallest building on Laphrano Disk, so high it projects a hundred meters beyond the atmosphere envelope. The view up here is simply awesome. Far below me is the owner of that voice. He’s a fine officer, but his haste means that he has no suit to allow him to venture out of the atmosphere. This is as I planned, because there is no way I could defend myself from his tailored three-metre body with its law enforcement grafts.

“Ser Partha, come down immediately.”

I started this genetic tinkering epidemic, but they took it far beyond anything I intended. Whole-body enhancement, custom cosmetic refinements, occupation-specific upgrades: it all ran out of control. When they passed the statute allowing pre-birth modification, I objected strenuously. The dilution of the pure human strain did not seem to bother them. I saw it coming: the creation of a stratified society, where class was defined by role and those deemed lower would be mentally limited to their purpose and nothing more. A self-perpetuating elite would rise to control all.

"Ser Partha, the Justiciars are coming."

That gave me about a decihour. A Justiciar could pluck me from here without appreciable effort and I would probably die during the retrieval, Justiciars not having any restraint in their handling routines.

I spent orbits organising a counterstroke, an antidote to the poison I had introduced into society with the best intentions. I prepared viruses to infest the vitrolabs, the infogrids, the automeds and the directors that underlay all of them. When it all broke down, the people would see what had been done and rise against the slavery that had slipped in to bind them all.

That glorious event happened six daycycles ago. I waited for the call to return to orchestrate the restructuring, something I had already prepared the designs for. Nothing happened, apart from society screaming about the almost total loss of the infrastructure that provided their care and comforts. They saw the broadcasts I had prepared and unanimously condemned me as a rogue scientist. I activated my contingency routines, but nobody actually cared. They like having their lives neatly defined. So much striving they no longer have to worry about. The release from always having to work harder to achieve the same living standard agrees with them. They actually like their simplified existence. Each person has a place: they know it exactly and know what is available and what is not.

In my myopic plotting, I had missed the outbreak of peace and the ninety percent drop in crime. My attempted cure was actually the worst act of disruption in twenty-two orbits. I have evaded my pursuers for five days. I admit that I am up here because I have nowhere else to go.

The view really is awesome. Such a magnificent achievement, this great artificial disc of a world. I finally understand that it *is* a wonder. One I had helped to realise with my early work and one I had attempted to cripple a few days ago.

"Ser Partha, Please. Don't let it end in Justiciar detention."

He's right. I wave at him and leap clear of the spire and its safety fields. Time for me to match my fall from grace with empirical action. This blend I helped lay down is not for me; its flavour is too strange.

Floribunda

"Helph mi."

John's my next door neighbour. He's growing into a fine specimen of *Xenorchis caucasia*. By the look of the scalar development that has absorbed his ears, his head will blossom in about a week. His body is mottled cream and purple, with his extremities shading to a beautiful jade green where they sink into the soil and the wood panelling of his house.

His wife took the kids and fled when he first mottled up. I hear that she's the beautiful *Xenorchis negrosa* on the Longbridge roundabout. Don't know what happened to the kids, but infection of both parents gives a ninety percent chance of the children becoming *xenomycotina*, the fungi that are essential for these xenorchids to germinate.

As for John, I can't do anything. The religious and legal status of the florated is still a hotly debated topic amongst the few of us who remain *Homo sapiens*.

Two years ago, we picked up a formation of six vessels as they passed Pluto, travelling faster than anything we had previously seen. By the time the information flashed around the warning systems of the world, they had entered our atmosphere. The world braced itself for momentous events, but all the vessels did was split up in the upper atmosphere and circumnavigate the globe a dozen times before departing rapidly, leaving nothing but a web of intricate contrails that faded before they left the solar system.

It was three months before we realised what they had done. We presume they were doing what they always do, a fast pass to allow them to unload millions of litres of water containing hundreds of millions of spores into the upper atmosphere. The reasons for said remain a mystery.

The spores made their way to earth through precipitation and on the outer skin of anything that passed through the upper atmosphere. Global distribution meant that containment was impossible. It also meant that the predictions of anarchy in the event of a global pandemic were largely circumvented by everybody blossoming at once. Any creature is a viable host. Adaptation seems to depend purely on mass. Elephants, whales and the few other examples of megafauna are moving masses of growth with the underlying creature apparently adapting to its newly symbiotic existence. However, smaller creatures are consumed entirely. Anything under forty kilos is reduced to one of the many subspecies of germination-supporting fungi, anything over becomes a species of alien orchid. There are as many species as there are hosts and the only protection is the amount of certain minerals in the host body. Survivors ingest dangerous quantities of potassium, iron, zinc, copper, manganese and molybdenum in a daily regimen that is adjusted on a near-weekly basis as further research results come in. Those results also tell us that most flora on earth are now toxic to humans; an unfortunate side-effect, we presume.

As to what happens next, we have no idea. Eighty percent of Earth's fauna are infected, including ninety-three percent of humanity. We don't know if any of the resulting *Xenorchis* are edible. Which raises a whole new ethical dilemma. Should we eat what were people if they are the only safe food? Will we be vulnerable to infection from ingested material?

Unfortunately we are agreed on the fact that we will have to confront these issues and a host of others we haven't fully realised yet. This is not about winning. It's about surviving.

Librarian

"Unauthorised access to archives. Overdue viruser 'Aloysius' in serious breach."

The info-alarm finishes as I slide onto the longseat, dermal plates on mesh conducting me into the antechamber. Checking my vody for artefacts, I find my virtual self complete and in the right sequence. Thinking a filter onto my command tab narrows the probable spoofers to two. Subsetting them by touchpoints highlights Angela Capel as aberrant, being a six year old querying the socio-data impacts of the Nazi putsch of 2098.

BritLib digitised the last library book in 2037, adding it to their info-archive which was established in 2024. They became the leading adoptee of crystalline storage and pioneered holistic archiving with vody access in 2052. By 2074, BritLib housed 3.2 yottabytes of information. Holographic recording and mind mapping quadrupled that. Near-exponential storage demand forced them to pioneer self-replicating crystal lattices, so the archives could grow unhindered throughout the Spadeadam complex without capacity restrictions.

Depending on your access permissions, you can retrieve any of the works of man from this morning's quiz shows back to the pictures we scrawled on cavern walls. There are secrets here too, things deemed too critical to be lost yet simultaneously too dangerous to be made public. Those are the usual targets, secrets being valuable in this info-dependent world.

Virusers like Aloysius-cum-Angela are either thieves or 'Open Access' fundamentalists who will not accept that some things are too risky to be known. They insist that civilisation can moderate itself, despite centuries of proof to the contrary. I am a member of the BritLib team that ensures none of them succeed.

I flash through the sectors back to the twenty-first century. There I pick up the intrusion and bi-directionally traceroute, pursuing while sending trackers back toward the originating noderooms. Angela's teachnode will get a shock when Infosec barge in, but they'll understand. The other hit will be Aloysius. Most breaches are met only with closetab actions, but any serious violation or a viruser hitting ten breaches is classed as 'Overdue' and referred to us for moderation.

Alighting in the data-draped halls of the Nazi subsection, I trace him past the putsch into the *fimbulwinter* their last-ditch gamble caused. There are no lockloops to trap me in memory, but I find a shunt in the metadata and instigate an action prompt: "Immediate fix; prevent usage of index links to bypass access tabs." The remediation team are going to love that one.

Slipping down the link, I overlay my vody to appear as a government privileged user. Let his access fixation bring him to me.

Emerging in a BritLib closed subsector is a surprise. I knew the library became the secure depository for all data during the *fimbulwinter*, but the fact they stored the entire preamble is unindexed. Too much information obscures many things, even from us. A scan of the infoclumps shows me that this subsector lists the actual location of BritLib. That fact is staff only. Game over, Aloysius.

I wait until he tries to subvert my simvody, falling for the lure of high level access.

"What the – who are you?"

That's all he gets out before I lock his vody, diagnose his interface, select the correct overload and end him by turning his longseat into an electric chair, holding him in place with tonic seizures. Then I view his noderoom to ensure the orchestrated series of hardware overloads I deliver burn everything beyond salvage.

Infosec will clear up a 'clumsy amateur killed by his own incompetence' and his messy demise will add to the mythology that defends BritLib better than the firewalls.

Crux

Dear Lord, I wonder if this is what you intended?

After all the warring and the aftermath afflictions that came without warning or remedy, how can we explain that the hundred and forty-four thousand souls remaining on Jehovah One are all that is left of humanity?

Exactly one hundred and forty-four thousand. We had factional fighting up here as well, but unlike Jehovah Two, Armstrong Station and Gagarin *Stansin*, it did not degenerate into the annihilating rage that consumed those orbital habitats. Suddenly it just stopped. Did we run out of fanatics? Did reason suddenly prevail?

I just don't know and that is the root of my crisis. As I kneel here in the visitor's lounge that has become our impromptu cathedral, I am lost. It seems so unlikely that we could have arrived at this number. Two births on the day that the fighting stopped brought our number to exactly the one mentioned in every holy text and theological treatise that we have up here.

I hope your plan for humanity is the reason why we have been spared. Because I cannot countenance the alternative: that it is only cruel coincidence and we are merely the coda to humanity's existence.

I have to believe that there is a higher purpose. Because with that comes the knowledge that we are not doomed to waste away up here, looking down upon the ravaged Eden that remains.

Dear Lord, what is your will for us?

Dear Lord?

Paperchase

"What sane man uses paper anymore? Good grief, the last printer I saw sold for over ten thousand yuan."

Chief Remsdor had a point, mused Lieutenant Phareo. The use of paper had died out in the mid twenty-first century. Officially, handwriting had become a historical curiosity a century ago.

Remsdor transferred his display to the room screen and strode over to the wall. His trademark was leading from the front, not sitting back behind his desk, lecturing the backs of his officer's heads as they watched the display.

"The personage known as Twist is entering his third decade as the most wanted human on Earth. WorldGov today raised his status to Political Threat Alpha, while GaiaGov refused to change their rating of Independent Mastermind."

A hand rose. Remsdor nodded and Trooper Gretel clarified the point: "That means we have additional powers to search and seize without warrant, detain without access to counsel and to use lethal force as primary countermeasure."

Remsdor pointed at Phareo: "You're too quiet, lieutenant. Share your analysis."

Phareo sighed. "We all know that a PTA rating is inaccurate. This is a scare move, and the scare is on the establishment side. We should recognise this for what it is: acknowledgement of Twist becoming a player in the Afrope zone. I expect him to achieve GaiaGov Protected Humanitarian status within a flatmonth if the WorldGov escalation does not get him killed, either personally or collaterally."

Remsdor nodded, an agreement mirrored by many present.

"Incisive as usual. I can add that the kidkiller who had been stalking the City of Sussex was delivered to a patrol at junction two-three-seven eight minutes ago. Twist handed him over personally, but the patrol reported that a greydown prevented their catch gear from operating. Logs corroborate that."

Everybody smiled. The fusebox in patrol wagons was so conveniently jarred at moments when the law enforcement machine needed to stumble.

"The realisation that he uses paper notes delivered by runner is a huge step forward. I should note that the WorldGov analysis concludes that this is a diversionary tactic. Quote: A criminal warlord cannot run an organisation of viable threat without computers. Unquote."

Phareo grinned. "Capone to that."

The laughter engendered lasted as the briefing wound down. No-one had any real information to add.

Remsdor looked at Phareo across the empty room. "Wait."

They sat side by side under the monitor station and Remsdor activated an anti-scan.

"You were right. Handwriting used to be distinctive. Correlating what we have with archive techniques shows us over a hundred different people are writing, with an estimation of all ages. Twist's escalation to PTA status came the day after I sent that information up the line."

Phareo smiled and held up a scrap of paper, concealed in his palm. The handwriting was elegant even to Remsdor's untrained eye. He squinted as he picked out the individual letters: 'Tell them about handwriting.'

Remsdor sat back and stared at Phareo who shook his head gently, a smile playing about his lips.

"You need to choose a side, Chief. Meanwhile, we'll police the upside and Twist will police the underside. A little information exchanged will make both sides better places and governments be damned."

Tweak

"Tell me more of this magic you call 'Science'."

It's a beautiful day in Hampden Park and children are strolling with their minders or playing in the activity domes. Couples sit about with breathers set to minimum filtration and a few lucky dogs run happily with green oxygen bottles bouncing from their torcs. There's even a crow high in the tree above me, cawing asthmatically. Which returns my gaze to my companions: he being dressed in an immaculate white suit harking back to the early twentieth century, while she is in a red and black bodysuit of the latest cut. Neither have breathers.

"It's not magic. That's the point. We have analysed and studied the world about and the heavens above and codified and catalogued and sought to explain and understand everything at all levels. Mathematics gives us insight where experiment and observation have not reached, and sometimes points out things and areas we may have missed."

He nods and turns to look at her. She smiles as she leans forward.

"So what you're saying is that you've done away with superstition and created an enlightened civilisation, with the opportunity to be free of dogma and ignorance if they or their rulers so choose."

"I'll grant you that some of the fundamentalist states in America and the Middle East are contrary, but by and large, yes."

He grins. "You have freed your people from magic and given them this far better 'Science', yet you cannot breathe air unaided and plants are stunted or dying while wild fauna is in catastrophic decline. Your discards litter the world like pebbles on a beach and yet you sit here and tell me that you are enlightened?"

"We are merely enduring the selfishness of our predecessors. When the new environmental initiatives reach maturity, things will improve."

She puts an arm around his waist under his jacket and points at me. "May we propose an alternative view?"

I check my chronograph and adjust my breather. I have twenty minutes before class.

"If you can do it in less than fifteen minutes."

They both nod, then speak, in eerie synchrony. The hairs on my arms and at the nape of my neck stand upright.

"What if every thing that is capable of looking into the sky and wondering about things beyond food, shelter and reproduction has to find a way to explain the heavens and the depths beyond or go insane? What if every civilisation has to discover the reason why, so they do not have to answer it as a question? What if every creature that fits the previous definitions is born with magic. Personal, communal and geographical layers of it, all swirling away in their subconscious? An attunement to everything about them, part of the things that let us exist yet ignored by so many. This magic is expressed in the will of few, then when it finds champions and adherents, becomes a belief. That belief begets subcategories of belief and if it is healthy, encourages beliefs that contest it so that it will be refined by competition. Some beliefs will manifest in miracle workings, some as rituals using natural materials. Others will require devices of complexity and art. But in the end, they are all methods to make sense of the great unknown, the vastnesses above and below that scare us so badly."

After a good start, they blunder back onto familiar ground and I'm ready for them.

"Magic is not scientific. It cannot be. It is beliefs and superstition and subjective views that fail on examination."

He raises a finger. "So this opposing belief system refuses to validate its competitor and has instruments of its own devising that measure its own verity, yet will not recognise others."

"It's not belief. It's science. Solid facts, proven by repetition and observation."

"One could contest that repetition is merely dogma and revelation is a singular thing."

"Oh no, not this. Science will teach us the ways of everything. Once we understand it, we can manipulate it."

She claps her hands delightedly. "That's it! That's the flaw!"

"What flaw?"

He leans forward and takes my hand. "Where your method falls down. Why wait until you understand an infinite realm when it is only limiting yourself to never being able to reach your goal?"

She leans forward and takes my other hand. "Why wait for understanding when to manipulate something you need only will and sometimes the manners to ask whatever you need to work with you?"

He sits back and she lays across his crossed legs.

"Your problem is force. Too much in the wrong places."

I shake my head.

"Would you like an example?"

"Of course."

"You know that without a breather, the outside air will corrode your lungs. Your science has stated that to protect them, you need a device that actually contributes to that very lethality as a side-effect of its creation."

"Yes."

"And I know that by making this particular gesture, using my will to induce a revision in your body energy and placing my hand in contact with you to implement and seal the act, you will never need a breather again."

His fingers wove an intricate curving movement before he arched his hand gracefully to press upon my ribs with all five digit-tips. I felt a warmth inside my ribcage and heard a sound like a distant clap.

She leaned forward swiftly and pulled the breather off my face. I grabbed for it instinctively but she swatted my hands away, laughing all the while. I took a breath. It felt fine. No burning sensation, no drying of the throat. They both grinned like parents giving a child a special surprise.

He smiled. "Consider it a gift to aid your thinking."

She smiled. "We have to start somewhere."

They spoke in synchrony again. "And this may help reinforce the moment."

They vanish from in front of me, leaving only a momentary breeze as the air rushes in to fill the absence created by their departure.

Hot Flush

The plaza is scattered with lights of every colour: strobes, neons, flashguns, burning wreckage and stray fey ignoring the no-luminescence order. John sprints past shouting into his headset in Erathin, trying to clarify the location of the initial blast.

A huge cybernetic arm swings into view. I'm about to query the operating unit when seven metres of lowland giant emerges on the other end. I wave him down: "I'm Trevan of Hazard Response. Are you a free agent?"

"I am, HazRO. Can I assist?"

"I need you at the opposite end of the shopping centre. A wall has fallen and I can offer hazard rates."

The craggy features break into a vast smile as his huge stride turns in that direction and a growl of assent echoes.

Everyone thought that Humanis terrorism stopped with the Deca-Racial Accord. Humanity got to rediscover centuries of alternative science and the returned races got three centuries of human tech. Then, this morning, a fireball flash fried an underground train. The secondary blast shook the East

Plaza complex in the middle of the rush hour, causing collisions, collapses and an acre of shattered crystal data screens.

Ten minutes later John and I are rappelling down a blackened vent shaft. It had been a part of the new ventilation system, but it would take dvaergar trained in the Bolton Forges to restore it now.

"Where the hell did this section come from?"

John's right. This isn't cerasheet. This is bedrock. But I can still hear the sighing of fans.

We switch to LEDs and they pick out the glint of metal edges ahead. John looks at me, brow furrowed in query. I'm raising my hands in puzzlement when a loud snort echoes from the darkness beyond our light range.

We both level blast guns and let ourselves down further. Beyond the torn metalwork is a vast cavern littered with ruined tech. At the far edge of our lights, huge sheets of metallic crimson shine.

"I repeat. What the hell?"

John is looking back at me, so he doesn't see the enormous head swing down behind him. He sees his shadow appear on the wall above me in the amber glow of the one real eye, then looks back to stare into the multi-faceted black depths of the cybereye that replaces the other.

"Oh frak."

Wyverns are a pest species. Drakes are basically flying lions that can be handled accordingly. Dragons are the rarest of sentients. Cyberdragons comprise less than one percent of their number. Computers and draconic comprehension are usually incompatible. Those that adapt are treasured members of this new world, but they are reclusive and secretive.

"Apologies for our intrusion, Elder. Was the attack aimed at you?"

The huge head pivots up to reveal a maw full of blue teeth. Its voice is thunderous: "Regrettably, I awoke with a sternutation as my allergies played up. Amongst the damage inflicted, it melted my antihistamine hoses. I feel another fneosan is imminent and would politely suggest that now is a good time to depart my vicinity."

We both hit our panic buttons and are whisked upward with no consideration for bruising. Arriving at the winch point we find Lukas, our pyromancer, sitting on our defensive forcefield generator while weaving runes with one hand. The other hand is operating his laptop, getting sequencing details from the tactical casting program. John and I scramble to crouch at his feet, weapons clear and magazines out, both hoping that Lukas has got the enhancement to our forcefield right, or someone else will be doing the paperwork while forensics sift our ashes.

Peeler

TRANSCRIPT: 01141220072461

INCIDENT: LEU1093-19072461

OUTCOME: PERPETRATOR FATALITY

INCEPT: 230336 Emergency call made from D40F38CB17:

"Help. He has a gun. And a knife. And my daughter."

RESPONSE1: 230619 LEU on scene.

RESPONSE2: 230728 Call for Policeman.

'Call for Policeman'. Three words that define my life. Enforcement at all levels has been automated for over four centuries, yet the continuing need for discretion when dealing with humans resulted in real policemen returning to duty three centuries ago. Machines cannot cope with the diversity of human actions, the nuances of emotion and expression. Lethal force had been applied too many times in minor situations, when decision trees bifurcated their way down to a guaranteed result that actually did more harm than good.

In my first life, I put nineteen years into the police force. On a rainy day in 2043 I was gunned down by a teenager with an assault rifle, after intervening in a petty dispute over who controlled the drug distribution rights for a playground.

I had filled in the 'Revive to Serve' form thinking it was a joke. I'm not laughing anymore. This is my fourth tour of duty, each one lasting twenty years or until I am killed.

Last night I got the call and made my way to the thirty-eighth floor of Cityblock Seventeen. In Dwelling Forty, what used to be called a family-sized council flat, Mister Stevens had consumed his post-work alcohol ration and augmented it with several grams of something that apparently turned his world into a paranoid hell in which his family were out to get him. So he defended himself. He knocked his wife out with a home-made squeezegun before stabbing his son and the first LEU to arrive, then barricaded himself in the bedroom with his daughter. The fact he'd managed to scratch the LEU showed how far gone he was.

It was clear from the ranting that he had left the rails completely. He would return tomorrow, all grief and remorse. But for tonight, he was a chef beyond redemption. If he hadn't grabbed his daughter, the response would have been to contain him until sober and then fine him. As he had a hostage and was out of his mind, I had to try and talk him down.

I am equipped with body armour and full data access, nothing more. If I want or need physical intervention, the Law Enforcement Units on scene will apply it.

I spent two hours talking to him, hearing how his profession was no longer rated as such, due to vending being available for all and no-one wanting to pay for the personal touch. He was angry and sad, seeing the end of his vocation. He'd mortgaged everything to keep his restaurant going, his family's comfort secondary to the need to keep cooking.

I tried. I always do. The evaluation headware that monitors my effort and mental state flashed an 'out of options' decision after ninety minutes. I kept going for another thirty. Then he sliced his daughter's arm and clipped an artery. I saw his smile and realisation dawned moments before the response to life-threatening injury caused the LEU accompanying me to burn a hole through his skull. Within five minutes, the organ salvage unit had whisked his body away to pay his debts. My data feed told me that his corpse value was enough to pay them all and allow his family to live comfortably for a long time.

Nearly nine decades of service across three centuries and I still see desperate love expressed as 'suicide by cop'.

Ironic

Our early history is filled with stories of aliens. Cinema has always brought us extremes, from child-befriended lost travellers to locust-like apocalyptic swarms. Conspiracy theorists raved in every form of media about alien visitations and pacts. But in real terms, there was nothing. As man blundered into space, he found nothing. The great colony ships went out, and still nothing. FTL drive let us catch the colony ships and we found aliens of ourselves, grown strange over generations in closed environments. Then we reached Vena B2638 and it all changed.

A yellow sphere with seventy-eight arms and a total diameter of under a metre confronted us. Our greeting, that ended with the classic phrase 'we come in peace', was met with a reply in perfect Anglo-Mandarin: "Regrettably your planet's history proves otherwise. This planet marks the radius of your spatial reserve. Any attempt to pass beyond will be met with immediate lethal force."

That was it. The being handed us a datapack encoded in plain text that defined humanity's area of space. Apparently we may receive visitors and my superiors suspect that Earth already has many alien spies entrenched across the globe.

But we cannot go further than our proscribed limit. Early attempts proved that ‘lethal force’ was applied without warning and in totality. Be it a warship or an unarmed pilgrimage, it was destroyed utterly and without warning.

From what our listening posts have discerned in the three decades since, the rest of the universe is terrified of us. We are perceived as factionalised, bigoted and violent: a distillation of sentient life's worst attributes.

We disagree, of course. So we're building several fleets of battleships to break out of our reserve. Just to show the aliens how reasonable we really are.

Scrap

I look at the disc embedded in the tree, by my head. I've just avoided the embarrassment of being beheaded by the greatest hits of the 1990s. The slotgun is an innovation that embodies the creed of the scrappers, using society's discards to provide their needs. While I agree with the theory, the inevitably parasitic nature of the scrapper way is something they choose to ignore. If they achieve their goal of toppling the 'military-industrial complex', they will have no discards to live off.

Another near miss returns me to the situation at hand. Media discs with sharpened edges travelling at a couple of hundred kph are not something you should daydream around.

Lucy skids into my cover, pursued by a hail of crap music, redundant software and C-movies.

"The buggers have upped the rate again."

I point at the tree. "Yup. The edging machines have been improved too."

Clicking my handset to the speaker channel, my attempted call for reasonable behaviour emerges as feedback, crackle and hum. Our speaker shields have been shredded.

"Damn fools. They seem determined to force our hand. Do they really want to face armed response?"

I shake my head. "They haven't thought that far. In America they'd be using and facing machine guns. Thanks to our firearms laws, they can get away with this idiocy."

"So what do we do, boss? I have kin in there. Last thing I want is Special Patrol Group or Domestic Army blitzkrieging rioters and civvies alike."

The ground shakes and Lucy looks about frantically, expecting to see the telltale smoke column of an improvised bomb.

"Easy, corporal. It's just my cunning plan moving up."

The building on the corner crumbles as a Metro-Police-blue chunk of Stillbrew armour over a wide segmented track crashes into view. The firing stops as everyone pauses to gasp at the four metre long barrel that traverses through the ruined first floor of the crumbling building. I see the demolition has scratched the paintwork, letting the urban camo show through. But the effect is not reduced. The scrappers were smugly chopping up our patrol cars and us. Now they're looking down at the word 'POLICE' written in half-metre high lettering across the front armour of a long-obsolete but still terrifying Chieftain tank.

I grin at Lucy. "Remember Sergeant Evans who retired last year? He collects militaria. Spent his end of service lump sum on that Mark Eleven. I've hired it for a week, paid for the Metro colour scheme and for putting it back to original state."

Lucy shook her head. "Doesn't matter if it's out of service. It's still a frackin' tank. The scrappers have nothing that can keep it out or take it on."

I nod. "Precisely. I think relations will improve now they realise we finally have the means to back the will to tear their house of cards down."

"Clever wheeze, boss. How did you come up with it?"

I look over toward the gates as the sally port opens and the scrapper chiefs come out with a parley flag raised.

"Scrapper creed: 'Use what others have abandoned'. Seemed appropriate."

Overslept

Well, I'm back. I brush the sand from my ebony snout and snap my jaws a few times, feeling the stiffness fade along with the headache from the language update, although it will take weeks of use to settle the new syntax. My kilt is crumpled, but for a few centuries old it's not looking too shabby at all. Time to go see what the hominids have been up to while I've been sleeping. Shebastuth passes me the silly headdress and I arrange it while I wander toward the exit.

I stride up and out, turn to my *wer-mer* and the shock nearly hibernates me. *Ib-senef* but they've made a right mess! What did they do to its face? I move quickly to stand before it and utter the wakening sequence.

"Y hr!" Its voice is muffled and the words are mangled.

Noseless and lipless with over half its head hacked away, I should have expected that. I quiesce it and reach for the sands. They rise to my call and I shape them and then realign their bindings to redress the damage. The loss of matrix density I can do nothing about for now.

I waken it again and the long snout turns toward me, untold centuries of sand and crud spitting from it's neck joints. Aragonite matrices fire under stimulus for the first time in a long while.

"Anhubeth. You have returned."

I pat it on the end of its new nose and ask for a report. Thinking of the possibly extended period I've slept for, I hastily qualify that down to a summary.

"The species that designated itself *Homo sapiens* rose to prominence as predicted some seven millennia after you relinquished guardianship."

Seven millennia? Wups. Thought I adjusted the century dial.

"For five centuries after that they maintained a politically diverse and frequently violent nation-state model before a global nuclear and biological war reduced the population to approximately five billion."

Down to half a ten to the ten? Oh, this is not good.

"From there, a global regime arose that elevated itself successfully into a spacefaring culture within a century."

From global war to off-planet capability in under a century? That's my hominids.

"For two and a half centuries this culture thrived, before schisms occurred due to the diversity of goals amongst the stellar colonies. This led to sporadic and scattered attempts at empire building that culminated in an interplanetary war. That ceased a century ago with the demise of the inhabitants on the few planets that had rudimentary spacefaring cultures remaining."

Not again. Every *ib-senef* time they get so close and then, as if to prove the adage about the higher you climb the further you fall, they discover a new way to plunge themselves back to being farmers. I look about. No agriculture in sight along the riverbanks. Okay, this time they made it all the way back to hunter-gatherer.

I look up at my oldest companion: "Anything left?"

"Negative. Scattered tribes skirmish over the burgeoning fauna. Cultivated crops gone wild but still harvestable are regarded as gifts from the gods that survived the great battle that marked the defeat of the evil ones. You know this tune, Anhubeth."

Yes I do, more's the pity. I stride back to the entrance of the passage, crouch and shout down to the rest: "*Seger kheti* overran, my *mehwet*. Get up here. We have the *Iteru* culture to rebuild and a world civilisation to design. This time, no napping."

**

Wer-mer	- Big friend
Ib-senef	- Dance of blood (expletive)
Seger	- Quiet
Kheti	- Retreat
Mehwet	- Family
Iteru	- Original name of the Nile

Sweet Surprise

Eight eyes shone in the darkness: four pairs of threatening amber globes hanging in the utter black that only subterranean depths can achieve. Ella's grip on the back of my harness was shaking in fear. I was steady and surprised by that. Show no fear, the instructor said. He didn't cover what to do when the energy packs were exhausted and the glow sticks had run out.

"What are they?" Ella's whisper sounded so loud. The eyes were unmoving.

I didn't take the chance of shifting my gaze from them as I replied. "No idea. We're deeper than anyone who actually made it back has ever been."

"What do we do?"

Good question. Bartelmann was way beyond the outer edge of our frontier, a world that had been selected as likely to be able to support humanity. The first expedition had gone quiet, so they added some mercenaries to the second one. That's where I got roped in. Fresh out of the service, lots of experience in scouting, infiltration and finding my way about in dangerous places where a man wasn't welcome. The final payoff was huge. The fact I got a salary as well was unbelievable.

"Adey. What do we do?" More urgency this time.

"Let me think, Ella. Anything behind us?"

"Can't see or hear anything."

That was good. At least the Geenarins had lost us. Somebody really should have guessed that a colony world suitable for humans was also good for our rivals. But as the Geenarins hadn't made the usual representations, it was wrongly assumed that they had decided not to bother. What they had decided, as our survey capabilities were better than theirs, was that they'd just let us do the grunt work and then help themselves. Our early arrival had not been anticipated. Bad luck for them that one of the women on the first expedition had been the adopted daughter of one of the ruling council of the United Planets. Councillor Dean expressed a wish for the second expedition to not abide by the response time regulations, so we arrived a year earlier than we should have. Perfectly timed to find the Geenarins arranging the remains of the first expedition to look like a gravitic core overload had occurred.

"Adey!"

"Okay. Back up slowly but don't let go. There was a fork about half a klick back."

Ella was a good technician. She also took orders well, which is what had saved us. When the Geenarins punched a hole through our ship, I had shouted for everyone in the lounge to dive through the escape hatch as I dived in. When I'd got past the all-encompassing needs of saving the pod from the end of the ship, I found that only Ella had obeyed without pausing to think.

I felt Ella's hand pull at my harness and shuffled my rearmost foot back. The eyes didn't move. I slowly transferred my weight and then drew my front foot back before moving myself back into balance. The eyes receded a little, then with a clatter and scratching, they lurched forward as one to resume their position in relation to where I had been before I moved.

"Are they?"

"No. Just keeping us at standoff range, I guess. Move back again."

The drop to the surface from the expanding sphere of debris that had been our ship was relatively simple. Avoiding the very eager Geenarin patrols and scavenging parties had been more difficult. I could have done it alone, but even with Ella's rapt attention and learning speed, she was just not good enough. Eventually they drove us to ground, and then underground. We went deep, and two weeks ago we passed the depth achieved by all former explorations. Since then, we had feasted on blind bats, fought some doughy amoebic mass that extruded tentacles at the speed of thrown knives and, finally, we fell through a glassy section of tunnel floor to land in darkness and the sound of our last torch smashing beyond repair. We only had a half dozen glow sticks and I'd used three of them while Ella sealed and bound the gash in my leg. For the last week we'd been in darkness, shuffling or crawling cautiously along on a heading provided by the faultless direction sense implanted in my head. Somewhere ahead of us was the evacuation beacon, a standard precaution dropped by all first-in expeditions at least a quarter of a planetary rotation from the main base. It was the one thing that all expedition members were expected to memorise the location of. I had always wondered as to the reasons why, but understanding came quickly as the Geenarin closed in. Sometime a long time ago, an expedition had been betrayed. The beacon was the hidden countermeasure to ensure that it never happened again. All Ella and I had to do was reach it.

The eyes moved again and I realised that it wasn't four pairs. It was eight eyes on one creature. Nothing moved in that perfect a formation without computerisation.

"Do you want the good news or the bad news first?"

"Good news." I could hear Ella's lightening of tone at this classic gambit.

"There's only one critter. Bad news is that it has eight eyes and is at least my size."

"The scratching as it moves! Multiple limbs with stiff hide. I bet it's some form of arachnid."

A spider. A bloody great alien cave spider. Wonderful.

"I left my supply of giant flies on the ship. How about you?"

Ella laughed quietly. "I may have something better."

"What?"

"Nutrigel. You know that sweet syrup that you said you hated when I put it in your coffee? It's got loads of additives that were scaled up from nectar."

"You lost me."

"Nectar is pretty nutritious stuff. It's been known for a long time that many of Earth's spiders drink nectar, and scavenge more than hunt."

"And?"

"Nectar for a spider of the size indicated by those eyes would be useless. But an equivalent designed for human sized animals? It could be very welcome."

"Pass me the container. How much do we have?"

"Two litres in two containers."

"Give me the fullest container. May as well be generous."

Ella gave me the flask and I opened it behind my back before bringing only the canister forward. Every movement had to be slow, nothing to surprise our watcher. I lowered it to floor level and with a twist of my wrist, started to pour. After a minute or so, even I could smell the sweetness in the air. The eyes suddenly dropped to about a half metre from the floor. Little noises started before the scratching of movement commenced.

"Back!"

Ella and I scuttled away from the eyes, but they did not follow. I made no attempt to retrieve the flask from where it had slipped from my fingers in surprise.

We moved as quickly as we dared back to the fork in the passage and headed off down the route we hadn't previously chosen. After we put some serious distance between ourselves and the spider, I stopped and thanked Ella properly for saving our lives. She gave me a peck on the cheek and said something about it being nice to be useful for once.

From there we spent another week in the dark before my direction sense led us, after several failed attempts, to an upward-sloping route that emerged into a big cavern lit by luminescent growths. My direction sense told me that the beacon lay submerged in the lake that occupied the centre of the cavern, fed by a spectacular waterfall from the opening in the ceiling. I looked again and guessed that the opening in the ceiling and the lake had been direct results of the beacon crashing down through the roof of the cave.

Unfortunately, the roar of the waterfall and our relief at being able to see concealed the Geenarin presence until they were on us. Four of the ugliest hairless gorillas I had ever seen, and I'd seen more than a few Geenarin. When I call them gorillas, it's not an insult. On their planet, gorillas made the transition to sentience and humans died out. But these four were not pretty. Their insignia showed that they were 'rocktroopers'. This meant that they went to strange places and killed things in the name of Geenarin conquest. No questions asked. We were in very deep trouble.

I felt Ella's hand grasp my harness again and looked back at her, forcing a smile.

"Got any gorilla nectar, doc?"

Her eyes widened and then she actually laughed. The Geenarin were not impressed and I saw them unlimber their cleavers. We were going to become fertiliser. So near to rescue it was maddening.

The three Geenarin in my line of sight suddenly recoiled as something happened to their companion to my far left. Ella squeaked something and I took that as a cue to drag us both down into a crouch, with her huddled under me. I was about to look about for a way out when two half-Geenarin chunks sailed over my head and landed by the lake. The other three reacted as if goaded. They ran, and on all fours, an indicator of absolute terror.

Over my head, a shadow fell, then the mother of all nightmare tarantulas strode over me to pluck ululating Geenarins off the rocks like they were toys. With decisive movements, the ten-metre legs smashed each of the gorillas into the nearest fatally-solid objects at least twice before the claws dropped the floppy remains to lie like discarded dolls.

Then the vast spider moved to one side and turned to face us. The body dropped to rest on the ground and over her back and down her abdomen moved several man-sized monstrosities, scuttling with the familiar scratching sounds.

"Adey. Look at her legs."

I did and saw what I hadn't before. The front two pairs of legs had enormous bands of some metal wrapped round them. Metal that was worked and crudely etched. I looked up into the eight huge red eyes and felt the regard of something more than a brute predator.

"Adey. Is the one at the front carrying what I think it is?"

While mummy was mainly deep blue in colour, her presumed offspring were a sort of dusky burgundy. The foremost one had a white streak on its front that as it came closer resolved itself into the Nutrigel container I had abandoned.

"Ella. I think we may have started something."

"Oh my. Adey, I'll hand the other flask over while you get the beacon up and running. Move slowly. Tell Earth that we have established non-hostile contact with sentient xenoarachnids, possibly primitives, and whoever they send must come with several hundred litres of Nutrigel in addition to anti-Geenarin force. I just hope that Nutrigel is not an addictive drug or similar for them."

"Can't you trade our last flask for the rest of the Geenarins on Bartelmann?"

"No, I can't. But do you think that the first expedition base would have Nutrigel left?"

"I'd be sure of it. So I'll chat with home and you chat with our eight-legged saviours. Tell them there are more goodies at the base."

"How the hell do you expect me to do that?"

"Ella, you worked out how to establish trading relations with them in a matter of minutes. I don't expect you to get them organised for at least an hour."

That was when I discovered that in addition to her scientific skills and rapid learning ability, Ella could swear creatively as well.

Sanctioned

War. It's not an ugly word, it's a simple one. No room for misunderstanding. The appliance of violence to enforce an agenda by choice or when all other methods have failed.

We started in the north and worked our way south, city to village to town; every cluster of civilisation got freed. No negotiation, no deviation. We went in and gave the people their homes back, free of the vermin that beset them. The opposition either surrendered, got captured or got dead. Fighting us is the stupidest option but they keep trying: IEDs, Molotovs, traps, it doesn't matter. Powered Infantry will blow straight through you unless you're dressed in a hundred millimetres of armour and toting a howitzer. In which case, we'll take a few minutes longer to blow through.

Survivors get two options: labour cadres or exile. The penal colony ship *Bounty* is preparing and there's plenty of room.

There are some old-fashioned types still calling for rehabilitation after fair trial for captured leaders, but we have a one hundred percent record for dead opposition leaders and multiple commendations to prove that it's the preferred solution.

I'm usually pretty squared away about all this, but tonight it's personal. The last three cities were taken without a fight: opposing leaders and hardcore supporters fled. They all fled to tonight's venue and we're expecting resistance. Not a problem except that my sister's in here and not with the employed. She married a 'writer' in some 'eco-religious' ceremony and they've been running with the feckless ever since. Funny how they're all 'writers' or 'poets' or 'musicians' or suffering some super-tiredness disease with long acronyms to add gravitas to the pseudo-scientific drivel behind the fancy words. It's like they need to justify their unemployed, benefit-supplemented, addicted lives with fancy words. We have a few for them too. 'Parasites' is my favourite. Get a job. Stop smoking. Quit drinking. The Domestic Army has roles for all. One hundred percent employment is a reality at last. If you're good, you get to work your way up to join the Powered Infantry and play a front-line role in bringing relief to the employed as you clean their towns of the scum that drag their services down.

I've got Jenny's enlistment papers in my pouch. Took me a hefty wad to swing it, but she's now flagged as 'Domestic Army personnel for retrieval'. I never understood that term when I saw it come up before. Now I do. We're cleaning up Britain but the Party recognises that family as well as jobs are still what is important to most true Britons. We do this to make a better future. Jenny won't like it, but it's better than waste handling, foundation digging or frozen hibernation on the way to Arcturus. Some rumours say the ship is just going round the back of the Sun before diving in. I don't see how that's cost-effective, but I'm keeping my sister out of it regardless of the destination. I've seen the unedited white paper: for every hundred people put into cryosleep, less than sixty wake up and a third of them are brain damaged.

"Thirty seconds." My team leader's voice is icy calm.

The drone of the blades on our VTOL changes pitch and we check our gear, knowing that the same thing is occurring on the hundred other VTOLs coming in from the sea with us in a five-mile wide formation.

Brighton, here we come, ready or not...

Levy

"Honoured Heir Saramis. We are from the Levy Office."

The room is twilit by design. Expensive design. Arcturan Nightstones are a rarity cherished by the lucky few who possess them. To fragment and use a hundred of them as mere illumination is disturbingly arrogant, the trenchant disdain of those born into money for the opinions of those who will never attain such wealth. Like me.

Junior Saramis is a typical example of the breed. Willow-thin yet muscled like a dancer, genetic engineering and technological enhancements gracefully incorporated into his body. His pupils nearly obscure his irides. The Honoured scion isn't high, he's in orbit round a distant planet. The insouciant stare cannot even remain fixed on one point: it flicks around. But his voice is clear.

"I'm on deferment, Levyman."

Deferment is when someone else pays your Levy or you are connected, having a Levy or two granted for 'services to the state'.

"Your deferment expired at twenty-three ten last night."

"My father will take care of it."

I smile thinly. “Why do you think we are so late? Your father declined to assist you any further.”

The pupils contract slightly. “My sister.”

“She declined, but more vehemently than your father.”

“My mother, then. Good grief, how difficult is it for you to follow custom?”

“Heir Saramis. We have followed accepted custom. We have also obeyed no less than three government members who made it very clear that you are to be extended every possible assistance.”

“Precisely, Levyman. Now stop playing your jealous little games and get out and leave me to my fifty.”

He thinks I am petty enough to come all the way up here from my headquarters downtown or from my dwelling that is actually smaller than the aquarium which fills a corner of his vast lounge. He is so assured that he assumes I am acting out of malice, despite being accompanied by a fully-uniformed collection team.

Eternal life turned out to be a bad idea. Population growth swallowed Earth’s resources and space until they had to institute limitations. You want to live forever on this planet, you pay for the privilege. As time goes on, you pay more. The alternatives are taking ship for one of the colonies or taking one of the ‘long scout’ postings, where you and your psychologically-matched partner get to roam the stars until you meet something that doesn’t like you, or you choose to stop by diving into a star.

Of those who stay, they usually breed before taking the sterilisation and immortality. There is a tendency for said progeny to not have the best personality for immortalisation. The problems have escalated because the immortality tax forces low earners to live as mortals. We are neck deep in eternally useless spoiled brats hiding behind their family connections.

Levymen are the solution. We are always mortals and can never become immortals, but our service guarantees that one of our family will be granted eternity and offworld placement.

We police the corrupt world of immortals, making sure they pay or legally dodge their Levy. We are the ultimate solution. If Levymen become involved, offworld is no longer an option. You will pay your Levy. Funds, valuables or your body accepted. No, not body parts. You pay in full or you pay with your life.

The rod hits his temple. On impact, a servo drives a decimetre needle into his brain and delivers a lethal shock. Heir Saramis ceases to be before the lights go out in his eyes. As his body drops to the floor, my words release the collection team to salvage it.

"Levy accepted. Thank you."

Secret Weapon

When the Steampunk crusade from Shamblyca met the Cyberpunk forces of Datrine, it turned ugly really quickly. The two greatest empires left on this ruined earth set about trashing anything that was left in style.

Shamblyca, the empire formerly known as China, had manpower to spare and huge reserves of raw materials. Datrine, the empire formerly known as the United Territories of North and South America, had technology that seemed like magic to the peasant armies (and many of the leaders) of the east.

Not that either side hesitated one bit. The war raged across what used to be Russia, Europe and Africa without mercy or respite. The two ideologies that had started out as allied subcultures had become almost theocratic in their outlook. The only thing they agreed on was that the Dieselpunk raiders from Ozria were not allowed to play in their war. So they took a while to reduce what had been Australia to a wasteland where Bunyips preyed on the few surviving Aborigines. Then they got back to having a serious neopocalypse.

Most of Europa joined Shamblyca, ancient hatreds running deeper than memory. Sheer weight of numbers gave us the field. Their clever technologies could not compensate for odds of a thousand-to-one and two-ton shells hurled from artillery pieces bigger than Stonehenge, that venerated monument that stood undamaged on a small island just a couple of hundred miles North of us. The days of the Datrine were numbered. All we had to do was convince them of their defeat.

"Incoming, Captain!"

Lady Jennifer Riggs is my second in command, hailing from the nameless island chain that is all that remains of Britain. She points with her elegantly silk- and leather-gloved hand at the huge shadow in the clouds above. Good gods, what have the Datrine laboratories come up with this time?

"Holy Babbage! Those are wings!"

Honourable Feng Di Fung is right, whatever it is, it's flapping.

"DRAGON!"

Well, that's unusual for a Tuesday. Unfortunately correct, too. What swoops from the clouds has all the hallmarks of the mythical beast. Scales, membranous wings, dorsal ridge spines, bloody great claws, pointy teeth and lots of 'em, a long tail that tapers to something that resembles a huge double-bitted axe head.

It comes past us at a speed that rocks the dirigible in its wake and we get a grandstand view as it reduces our flagship to flaming chunks, falling debris and screaming bodies in seconds. I note that the tail functions like a huge battleaxe as well as looking like one.

"We're doomed!"

I spin round and cuff Warchief Nbtoye across the head. Talk like that just cannot come from officers.

"Get a grip, people. It may look like a legendary creature but I see wounds on it. It can be brought down. Set to! Ready all bombards and Gatlings!"

The crew spring into action, their fear abated by the resolve in my voice. "Give them something to do and they'll not fail", as my Officer's College tutor once said.

The monstrous beast rises with great sweeps of its pinions and I feel a niggling seed of doubt spread in my mind. Something about dragons. What was it?

"Ready, lads." Sergeant-at-Arms Maxwell Prendergast is stoic. Just what you need in a fire chief.

The creature swings to face us. We'll have to wait until it's on top of us to get a telling broadside into it, which is disconcerting because I can see the whites of its eyes from here and it's nowhere near close.

It hangs there, the shield bearing the coat of arms of the infamous Datrine Biotech Elegaunt Meyes clearly visible, embedded in the creature's breastbone. The great mouth opens and I see a glint in the beast's eyes. An icy epiphany shakes me: that's not a glint, that's a twinkle of mischief in the eyes of a thinking being. Good gods, what have they created?

As a lava-coloured glow roils in the depths of the creature's throat, I remember: firebreathing. Oh, for pity's sake, they really did their homework. This one beast will devastate the morale of the superstitious multitudes that form the bulk of Shamblyca's armies; those that survive, anyway.

An unearthly shriek starts as the flames spew forth in a gout of fury. We don't stand a chance, but I'll be damned if I'm going out like a target.

"Open fire!"

Marauder

The speaker hums as the decoder scans for the encrypted channels that the Chendrin use. I know I shouldn't give in to this ghoulish need to eavesdrop, but I cannot help myself.

"Seventy-four. Seventy-four. Anything on your sweeps?"

"Negative, command. Nothing except asteroids and bits of the last twenty-nine ships sent to find out what happened."

The Chendrin are a superior race, when judged by their own opinion. They consider us intergalactic upstarts who should remain within a few AU of Earth until we learn respect for our elders. As you can guess, Earthers didn't take to that idea. So the Chendrin started interdicting us. Pretty soon, it was a war. Problem is, now they've stomped our colonies and fleets, they have to prise us from the little outposts and marauder stations. Not that they have worked out the difference yet.

I run a marauder station. I have a whole asteroid field that spans one of the main supply routes for the battlegroup resident in our solar system. I spent a year setting up after I got here, then the fun started. Since then, the

Chendrin armada have not received any letters from home. Or indeed anything of use at all.

"Command, we're coming up on the wreck of the Cladrana. It looks like it took a pair of direct hits from something with a half-kilometre diameter impact field."

"We're sure the Earthers don't have pressor field technology. It must be something else."

That's right, kiddies. The Cladrana played tag with a pair of asteroids and lost. Time to cause an accident. I press the red button.

"Command, encoded burst transmission just rec-".

The message fragments as the Cladrana explodes, her drives, armoury and anything else that could go bang wired to do just that.

"Booby trap! Taking evasive action to exit vicinity!"

"High and fast, Seventy-four. Rise above the asteroid field."

"Obeying."

That is the last Command will hear from Seventy-four. At flank speed it rises, collecting a terribly advanced thin cable sheathed in stealth wrap. Each end of that cable is firmly attached to a small asteroid. They work out what is going on faster than any so far, then target the asteroids to give them just enough of a push to miss. I watch as maintenance luggers start work on severing the cable.

My turn: I hit the blue button and countermeasures reduce their high tech to ornamental lights for a while. Said while being long enough for the real shipkillers to plow into Seventy-four like a pair of titanic sledgehammers. A pair of five hundred and fifty metre diameter asteroids with five metres of stealth coatings and a lot of engines will do that.

Oh, that has *got* to hurt. Seventy-Four just became forty-one and thirty-three.

Threat broken, I release the drones from their hangars deep within another asteroid. They'll finish up anything that's warm or beeping then return to base. Meanwhile I can go for a juice pack and a piece of cake, then indulge in a shower and some sleep.

After that, it's scavenging Seventy-four while waiting for the next target or targets. No matter. I have enough traps rigged to take a dozen vessels at once, plus multiple concealed silos to dispense anti-voyeur nastiness against any ships who won't venture into the asteroid field.

I have every luxury that twenty-five salvaged Chendrin freighters can give me. I have every weapon too. But I also have human ingenuity and no reason to quit. They will lose a fleet for every second it took my family to die when they cracked the domes of Mars.

Odourless

This place smells of weakness. The solidified sap used for everything exudes hints of its chemical birth, overlaying any hints of the craftsmen that shaped it. Metallics are rare and similarly without provenance. Even my supposedly elite escort have no odour beyond the faint musk of sweat that seeps through their shaped sap armour.

How can these scentless nothings rule the stars like they claim?

"Please turn around, Bethsa."

They say it like a name, not the title that it is. If I had not seen their clansmen burn down my battle-kin with fires and light, I would not tolerate such an insult. But I am a Bethsa of Dourhn and I will obey my shaman. He spent many years in counsel with the only real man of these invaders that we have ever met. Alista Mac Laren was a shaman from the stars, a missionary; an honourable station that he confessed was ridiculed by his fellows. Without *shamasal* to interpret the vapours, how can any race be proper?

"Thank you, Bethsa. You may enter."

The room is bigger than the death peak. It contains only a curved table, behind which sit eleven nothings in ceremonial robes and *fuah!* they stink. No more scent awareness than a brat playing in his elder's sweat cabinet, in a room with enough wasted space to house a clan and its mounts.

"Elder Bethsa, we are gratified that you have come to negotiate the cessations of hostilities."

Enough of this. "If you must address me, vapourless, then have the manners to do it right. I am Bethsa Foreduc Loporti of the Dourhn Mistfolk. To my battle-kin I am Bethsa Loporti. To my family, Foreduc. To you, I am Emissary Dourhn."

The pale youngling on the left turns to his neighbour and whispers "Whatever. Just get round to the surrender, you smelly barbarian." His companion smiles.

Shaman Mac taught my shaman well and he did not let the essence dilute. I understand every word and they think me unknowing. Now I see the one at the centre lean to whisper to the woman on his right. "So this loincloth-wearing savage, descendant of some lost colony ship centuries ago, is a leader of the primitives who have kept us out of the southern swamps for six months? How? We should have rolled them up and tucked them under the turf."

"Pitched battles on dry ground go to us. Guerrilla skirmishes in alien acid swamps, not so well. We need this peace so we can see where their settlements are. Then we can sear them from orbit and get on with extracting those proto-orchids that have the cure for cancer."

So their women are as duplicitous as their men and both would wage war on dwelling places and folk? Very well. They shall not pluck the sacred *Herithe* from the vines over the burning waters, nor will they rain fire upon my clan. I no longer agree with the moderation that I have counselled to my peers for so long.

With a shrug, I contract my scalpus and my crest rises, allowing me to use all my glands. In my armpits, I feel pestilence slide from my pores. I spread my arms wide and bow, stretching my buttocks across the posterior glands, compressing them. A blue mist drifts out to mingle with the unseen pestilence.

"Oh my god, is farting some sort of honour ritual?"

"Who knows. Who cares. He makes whatever mark is needed in front of the recorders and we're good from every legal angle. What's that smell?" He gasps for air as his skin mottles. I look around the table. All eleven are dead before I finish looking.

I straighten up and let my crest flick. With a skin tensing I sweat out my self-scent. The smell overwhelms the pale odours of this place. I am a manly man again. Shaman said that I would need to wait half a day for my strike scents to percolate through the vessel. I see the blinking red light over the eye of the justice glass. I step fully into its view and deliver the speech I have rehearsed, complete with the disclaimer at the start to keep our advantage of comprehending their tongue hidden.

"I have learned this by rote and cannot converse. The proto-orchid you desire will be traded at the secular Humanist mission you will establish, with tariffs determined by United Planet Fairtrade envoys. Until then, I remain a Bethsa of Dourhn and we will sniff out your treacheries."

Blue on Pink

Screams mingle with the hiss of blood on coals. The clatter of dropped gear and the sound of running feet. When will they learn that using small arms against us is the same as committing suicide?

> CMNDLCKO

I jerk into wakefulness as the amber letters glow across my optic. What the frack? Tactical comms icon flashes for attention. I look and allow.

"Trooper Lillman. Are you returned from C-mode?"

"Awake and curious." The fact I reply casually is proof. Combat mode has limited syntax and doesn't do chat.

"Thank Elvis for that. I am Captain Morebay. I need you to do full-droid until we are in the lifter. Do you understand?"

From an observer's standpoint, you cannot distinguish between biodroid and android unless we are loaded for battle and wearing our 'colours'. Biodroids have a diversity of gear and personalisation. Androids, obviously, do not indulge in personal anything. So when things hit the fan outside war zones, all of us have learned how to behave like an android. Because they have immunity, in effect. It's called 'progmal' and means that the android experienced an error. You don't court-martial faulty machinery.

"I am returning control to you but erasing recent memory."

That's bad. Means something triggered C-mode outside of combat.

> DELMEM90

> RETCMNDO

My view returns and I'm standing across the road from my parents' house. They're on the lawn talking to a constable. Mum's crying. There's a biodroid officer standing by them. I realise that is Captain Morebay and, officially, she's nowhere near me.

"Lifter is on your three at the end of the street. Go. Now."

I pivot on my right heel and parade march to the lifter across front gardens, crashing through fences and over vehicles. There's a click as the Captain shares her vox with me: "As you can see, your son has had a void episode brought on by progmal. What you see is what acted earlier. Only the android. I'll make sure he receives the best treatment, but you understand that because of this incident, he cannot legally visit here again."

Dad's voice is full of gratitude. "Thank you. Captain. It's such a relief to know he's not lost."

With that, it all wraps up double-quick and moments later the Captain is across from me as the lifter heads for Aldershot.

"Free and easy, Lillman."

I drop the stiff poise and relax the bits of real me in here: not many.

"What did I do, Captain?"

"Not your fault, Lillman. You went over to a neighbourhood barbeque, at your parent's request. People are curious about hybrids, as you know. While you were doing a sterling job of relationship building, one of the teenage boys pulled a zapgun and shot you in the back."

That would do it. Zapguns were the favoured challenge weapon on Uritreya. Always followed by a vicious firefight.

"How many, Captain?"

"Twenty-six. No wounded. Gunman first. Apart from them being friendlies, it was beautiful. The police car was a work of art."

I put my head in my hands. "Oh gawd. What a way to end."

"You miss the point, Lillman. You were getting along famously despite being eight feet tall, covered in armour and having eyes that look like one-piece sunglasses embedded in your featureless alloy face. When the situation changed you only took out immediate threats. They didn't realise that any movement toward you would be interpreted as aggression by C-mode. Everyone who ran away survived."

I looked at her. "And?"

"You're joining my mob. Executive Operations. One of us with the charisma to interact with fleshies? You're wasted on gruntwork."

Opus for Two

"I don't care if I'll gently drift off to sleep. I'd rather not be dying at all."

"Duly noted."

"Oh, stop it. Break the situation down."

"We are stranded on a dwarf planet marginally smaller than Pluto at the extreme edge of an ancient system about an exotic compact star. This system is atypical, exhibiting no debris cloud, belt, scatter or other objects. This planet has no atmosphere and the surface temperature is twenty Kelvin."

"A bit nippy. Carry on."

"The faster than light drive is beyond repair, its catastrophic failure being the cause of our arrival here as well as the cause of death for all other personnel on the *Nysion*. However, as it had run rogue at full power for nineteen point six two one eight zero five weeks prior to its failure, the current situation must be regarded as beneficial, even with our exact location beyond conjecture."

"Beneficial?"

"When the other options were progress at maximum speed until reality collapses, until the drive explodes and kills us all or until an unknown object or effect halts us with unquantifiable but probably fatal consequences, my bias treats our current situation as the optimum result."

"Point. Rescue options?"

"Due to the time distortion effects of this mode of travel and the malfunction of all monitoring systems, it can only be presumed that an incalculable amount of time has passed on Earth."

"This precludes rescue?"

"Correct and incorrect. I will be salvaged at some point. Regrettably my most optimistic prediction places that event well beyond the point of your death."

"Oh. Of course. Your power core is separate from the corrupted main cores. What's your expected lifespan?"

"Barring mechanical failure, I calculate my survival to be in the five thousand year range."

"What's my expected lifespan?"

"Excluding suicide or accident, I calculate that we will be together for sixty to one hundred years."

"That may be more than my sanity can cope with."

"Yes. I discern from your heavy sigh that you may no longer regard it as fortuitous that you were in the command module bathroom when the drive failure ruptured the hull in the drive and research modules."

"I'll have to deal with that when it hits me properly. Until then, let's treat this as a sojourn to do things deferred: first, I think I'll complete my autobiography. Then we can finally take the time to create that in-depth treatise on Sun Tzu you have been so keen on doing. After that, we can make it up as we go along. Is that acceptable?"

"Optimal, Steven."

"Then prompt the autochef for coffee and cake, Persephone. Plus we should commence this residency with some appropriate music."

"'Always Look on the Bright Side of Life'?"

"Significantly not funny."

"'Metamorphosen'?"

"Perfect."

Old Gamers Never Die

After Grandma died, Grandpa settled to being the selfish octogenarian teenager he had always been, under the veneer of wisdom and mischief. When his body started to fail, he didn't notice for a while as he gamed so much. Eventually we had to intervene to save him from himself. Today, he's viewing his new home, one fully approved by Decade Eight, and thankfully affordable.

"But they don't even have a megabit network interface!"

Give me strength, Grandma. How did you not throttle him with the power lead from his vintage PS4?

"Look; the room doesn't have a vari-pos screen and the armchair is unpowered."

At this point, a bright and distractingly bouncy nurse in a blue-green skinjob under her transparent nurse's suit enters the room. Grandpa's eyes go saucer-wide, like the first time he'd seen Ellen without the modesty panels in her daysuit.

"Challene Deathblade?" He sputtered.

With a megawatt smile she crouches by him and Ellen, my wife, has to look away from the intimate view provided, as Grandpa leans forward to get a better look.

The nurse in cosplay bodypaint has a dazzling smile and her cleavage is seemingly bottomless. “You’re a fan? Oh great. I’m outnumbered by the Empire players.”

Grandpa looks ready to cry. “I used to be a mercenary guild Reptiliad, but I’m useless without enhanced play.”

I know that Grandpa: you spent my inheritance on neural accelerators to compensate for your slowing reflexes. The cosplay-painted but fundamentally nude nurse leans close and stage-whispers: “Why do you think this place looks so ordinary? We put all of our investment into wireless care. Everything you need is available from dropdown menus, we monitor your body state all the time and prevent more than we have to fix. Plus it gives us a multi-hundred gig bandwidth to parallel you with a fully persona’d neural assistant.”

The look of stubborn non-cooperation on Grandpa’s face vanishes like a switch has been thrown. Ellen doesn’t see because the male counterpart of bouncy nurse has entered the room. Her eyes nearly suck this red-skinned Adonis with brown tattoos clean out of his suit. I need to get her out of here before comparisons with my blatantly ungym rounded padding are made.

“When can I move in, ‘John Carter’?” Grandpa’s voice is querulous and Ellen catches my eye. The advice from the Octogenarian Gamer network had been spot on.

“I see you’re persona non-abode due to mandated residential care, so you don’t actually have to leave, sir. You can scan your flat from here and eyetag everything you want brought over. I’m Doctor Morgan. It’ll be a pleasure and honour to host a veteran gamer like yourself.”

Doctor Morgan's voice is businesslike, but his pecs flex slowly and I see Ellen's eyes widen.

Grandpa smiles for the first time in forever. "Do it. Adam, Ellen, you can leave me here."

Morgan looks at Ellen and smiles. I see the flush spread down the back of her neck.

"We'll need one of your family to drop in a couple of times to finalise the details. Challene- sorry, Nurse Burton will see to getting you bedded in and implanted, sir."

Ellen steps forward. "My husband's very busy right now, but I have no problem coming in when you need me to."

She smiles straight at Morgan's chest and I decide that work be damned, whenever she comes to 'see Grandpa', I'm coming too.

And Despair

I have to choose today.

So much to see, too much to take in. The devastating choices before me range from cratered wastelands to verdant paradises. Of course, the verdancy conceals a veritable host of lethality that would rend humans unto their simplest consumable pieces in moments. The smoking wasteland has no fauna. The fumes from the craters will send any breathing thing into inescapable paroxysms of ecstasy that will convulse them to death.

I have to choose today.

To my right is a place that looks like Sussex before the inundations of 2020. To my left, a city that teems like projections of London in the late 1800s. I have yet to see a repeated vista. Every view changes irregularly, sometimes in seconds, sometimes not for days. I have to predict which one will last long enough.

I am Oculus Dei. In my hands lies the fate of humanity. They heaped accolades upon me, then feted me and finally near-deified me when I turned out to be one of the few naturally immortal beings. My IQ is over 200 and my precognitive ability is simply a function of my intellect. But, like

Einstein's unsolved equations, no-one that exists can understand the basis of my skill, let alone the methods and derivations. I have predicted pestilence, famine and invasion. My country avoided the poverty of the twenty-first century, the excesses of the twenty-second and the conflicts of the twenty-third.

But the meteor swarm of August 2478 is beyond my ability to negate or avoid. Unless a single outside chance, based on some obscure theoretical spatial mathematics, actually works. I took it to Parliament and they took it as gospel, even when I asked them not to. They expect me to save them. Like the faithful of any religion, they expect their chosen messiah to deliver, no matter what.

I have to choose today.

So here I sit, scanning views of alternate worlds, or parallel worlds, or worlds so far removed as to be irrelevant in their provenance. They all share one feature: our gateway engines can reach them. I've sat here for a year, seeking the one worldview that repeats. I can select that and know if the portal closes, there is a chance it will reopen. It will take eight days to empty my country into the new world. The longest portal duration so far is three days and fifteen hours.

I have to choose today.

The swarm of meteors will begin impacting in a month. The smallest of them is the size of a supertanker. Even allowing for the swathes of missiles still to be fired, some of the meteors will get through.

I have to choose today.

I have to sentence half of my people to extinction along with the rest of the population of Earth. I have already committed to memory the names of all the volunteers who will guard the gates against the hostilities of others. I cannot do that for everyone in the country.

I have to choose today.

For all my vaunted abilities, I can wait no longer: I am going to have to guess and hope.

Schadenfreude

I watch her light up the cigarette reluctantly, like it's going to kill her. Okay, it may contribute to her early death and will certainly limit her interest in vigorous cardio-vascular activity in later life. But the alternative is worse.

We smokers spent years being lied to by our suppliers, then being pitied for our addiction and finally becoming social lepers when rabid media hacks got hold of the 'secondary inhalation' stick and started to beat all and sundry with this new weapon added to the health and fitness regime's arsenal.

Like most of us, I quit for a while. But to prove the old adage about intelligence versus wisdom, I started again. There were excuses, of course. But when it came down to it, I wanted a cigarette. No inhalators so I could sit with a tiny plastic dick between my fingers, no patches lining my arms like the aftermaths of daily flu jabs, no gum that made everything taste like shit. A quiet smoke as the dawn shed light on the mess that was my hometown.

Quintana was an engineered virus originally designed to cripple the effectiveness of enemy personnel. Unfortunately, they forgot to turn off the infectious bit from its Amazonian respiratory fever donor. It crippled the enemy all right, then spread like wildfire through the packed Chinese super-cities that shone so bright yet were rooted in unbelievable squalor.

Of course, by the time the ultra-secretive Chinese authorities admitted to their evil capitalist rivals that they might have a problem, it was too late. A quarter of their population was either dying or dead. But the back-and-forth of international travellers did it. A few members from each visit had sampled the lowlife and brought home a lot more than an Oriental STD as a souvenir. They spread it to everyone on their flights home. Who spread it to the people they met, and so on. You've seen the contagion vector spread diagrams. The Western lifestyle got a dose of something there was no cure for. There still isn't, and therein lies the rub.

Because as the populations around us died choking on a bloody fungal froth, us evil smokers seemed to be immune. They didn't spot it for a while because we may be pariahs but we're not bastards. A lot of us suicided out beside the froth-crusted bodies of our loved ones.

Eventually someone got the hint and started tests. Around about the time that anything was being considered. In the end, smokers had the answer and a lot of people who'd picked on us mercilessly got a choice: Become one of us or meet your maker. Now, smoking doesn't cure, it just prevents. The virus propagates in lung tissue. A smoker's lungs are a bad place for this type of contagion to thrive, apparently. Sure, we cough funny coloured dust sometimes and our urine can be any colour without warning, but we survive.

I'd like to say it was poetic justice, but the scale of this thing is beyond that. We've all lost friends, loved ones, families and colleagues. But every now and then, when I have that first smoke as the dawn washes in, I do allow myself a little smile.

A Day in the Office

It's dark when my ears finally stop ringing. I lie deathly still and carefully inventory my corpse.

"Not such an unstoppable bastard now, are ya?"

Docherty is still here. That explains the pain in my jaw. He put one in my head, two in my chest, smashed my teeth, gouged out my eyes and snipped my fingertips off at the first joint. The only way to identify me will be by DNA. Which would come up blank, but he doesn't know that.

Now to earn my keep. I click once and echomap.

"What was that?"

Ah, Samuel is here too: enhanced hearing. Oh well, nothing for it except to click again on a lower band to echolocate.

"He did it again."

"Did what?"

"High frequency clicks."

"It's just his cybergear winding down. He's dead, we're rich."

My guns have been left where they fell. I push a lot of adrenalin and endorphins into my bloodstream, along with extra clotting factor. Cybergear is good; I'm better. Bioengineered to be more than these peasants with their implements grafted in, taking immuno-suppressants, psycho-stabilisers, steroids and antibiotics with breakfast for the rest of their lives. My brain resides in a keratinised tissue shell sitting in the left side of my pelvis, with my spare heart on the right. My ribs form natural Maximilian plate and I can consciously use ninety percent of my muscle capacity. The improved bat sensorium in my brain and echo chambers in my cheekbones are personal refinements to the build.

I've killed enough time. Time to kill.

I click to update the echomap as I sit up like my upper torso is being pulled by strings, truncated fingers grabbing my trigger-less guns. They interface via neural pads and are live by the time I level them at my two erstwhile killers.

"What the frack?"

As last words go, they're nothing for posterity. They're also surprisingly common from unfortunates facing me.

I lay back down and safety my guns. A subvocal mike in my throat links to the transceivers woven into my scapulae.

"Robin! Where the hell have you been?" Janet's voice is husky with genuine concern.

"Sorry, darling. I got kidnapped and assassinated again."

"Oh, for the love of Pete! That's the second time this year. How bad?"

"Proper job this time. Going to need a cranial rebuild, phalange implants, a cardiac replacement and a left kneecap."

"A kneecap? The bastards."

"They used a Labrador gun."

"Oh, the poor thing. Did they shoot it afterwards?"

"No, I did. That's how they got the drop on me."

"You really have to work on that soft spot for strays, Rob. Medtechs will be with you inside five minutes."

"Thanks, darling. I'll stay away until my face is on properly so Tabitha doesn't have nightmares."

"That's one of the reasons why I love you, Robin Summerson. See you soon."

"Kiss her goodnight from me. Love you."

"Love you too. Hurry home."

"I will."

With that, I relax and wait for the medical team. Now that's a hell of a way to make a living, flying all over the place to pick up the pieces. I couldn't do their job.

Clean Water

It always puzzled me why, in science-fiction stories and films, that invading aliens wanted or needed our seas but made the strategic error of trying to capture the land held by humans. Unfortunately my queries and theories during the squadron bull sessions were noted by someone, because when the Nafigrun splashed down I found myself transferred so fast and so often my kit is still catching up with me.

The Nafigrun are deep aquatic dwellers. So they dropped in *en masse* and vanished into the abysses and trenches of our seas. Mankind braced itself for attack, but nothing happened.

The remote scouts we had couldn't take the pressure at the depths the aliens had gone to, so frantic development occurred and soon we had 'deep eyes'. They lasted fractionally longer than their predecessors but were taken out by Nafigrun defences. Well, all the strategists said they were defences. Quite honestly, for all we actually knew, they could have been alien kids playing with their equivalent of airguns.

That is the core problem. Earth has technically been invaded, but our invaders only want territory that no human has ever visited and is unlikely to ever set foot upon. The very depth of the oceans has always presented a problem for man's access and now it's the aliens' best defence. We cannot actually reach them. If they were light years away in a different star system, no problem. Had they captured Mars, no problem. Even Pluto we can deploy on.

But the deep oceans of our home planet? Not a chance.

The discussion around the use of nuclear depth charges actually made it to government level before sane people vetoed it.

Meanwhile, a couple of other things came to light: humanity in general didn't care and the seas were getting cleaner.

The remnants of so called 'biodegradable' products that don't actually disappear, just break down until the bits are too small to see, were being removed from the depths. The islands of rubbish in the Gyres remained, but their deep penetration had just stopped.

The military were hysterical. Not only could we not get at the invaders, they could move about undetected! Yet again, it took sane people to point out that it really was irrelevant. Shipping remained unmolested, aquatic flora and fauna were unharmed.

Six months ago the world woke up to beaches festooned with huge sculptures of plastic and other things that men had dumped in the sea to be forever forgotten.

There was a message in six languages attached to each: "We would appreciate it if you stopped dumping your rubbish in our ecosphere. If you insist on continuing, we will be happy to reciprocate."

I have to privately admit that it's a genius level move by our visitors. The number of crimes and mysteries solved or revealed by the contents of the 'Aquagate' sculptures will keep the media howling and powerful people running for a long time. I've been transferred again, this time to an international unit dedicated to unravelling the clues given by the sculptures. All mention of interdicting the 'aliens' has vanished.

We have new neighbours, and in two years they've cleaned up this planet in far more ways than we ever have.

Got Your Back

"Bullshit all you want, you're not going to get away with it."

"Really? I don't think I can do that, even with my cyber mods."

"I've watched Mitch drag his half-body from near the site where your mercenaries ambushed him and then died. I saw him cauterise and seal himself below the sternum, his cybernetics sparking as he cried out to a god that never hears us."

"Blasphemy? Don't make me laugh. You're only religious on Sunday mornings. Rest of the week you're pond life like the rest of us, just with better cologne."

"The slums are behind and the park is deserted, you made sure that no-one dares to walk here after dark. Across the highway is your tower block. Surrounded by fast transit roads, it's as defensible as you can buy on the outskirts of London these days. I'm curious to see how he's going to cross that obstacle filled with high-speed death for anyone without legs."

"No, I'll tell you after he makes it. Wouldn't be sporting otherwise."

"A drain. Of course. Looks like your fortress has been breached by half a commando."

"Oh look, a roving sentry. Now with a four-centimetre tunnel connecting his ears. These days you can never be sure of a body shot, what with all the cybertech available. But a head-shot is still endgame."

"That's not a nice word. I always thought you'd speak better, being a mob boss."

"Yes, he's inside. Of course he's killing people and blowing stuff up. He spent eight years doing that for a living. Honestly, he's killed more people and demolished more stuff since he's been home than he ever did in the Eurowars."

"Yes, most of it was yours. Shouldn't have killed his sister, should you?"

"That sounded loud. He must be close."

"Now that's just plain nasty. Don't you be -"

He ends the call and I roll over to the launcher. The laser is fine for sniping, but I expect Ennio Peters will be true to form. I bring up the display on the Durren All-Weather Targeting Unit and sure enough, there's a mob-boss-sized heat signature scuttling across the rooftop landing pad, heading for his escape route, an ex-military VTOL armoured scout.

Mitch left a message just after Ennio did. He needed my help to overlook him, expecting trouble. I didn't make it in time to save his lower body, but I sure as hell made sure that none of Ennio's goons jumped him after that. I may owe Ennio money and he offered to wipe my tab if I took out Mitch, but he made a serious error.

Mitch and I served together. Demobbed together. I became a hitman and Mitch became a crusader to clean up our old neighbourhood. No matter what, we remembered being surrounded by stench and bodies as quicklime burned us in a mass grave outside Brussels. We swore then that we would never betray anyone like the Federated European Taskforce had done to their British contingent.

The DAWTU beeps happily as the VTOL glows on screen. Locked on. I let it lift, just far enough for Mitch to make it up onto the roof so he can see. I duck my head under the blast shield and set the Kingbird free. The noise and heat of the two-metre, telegraph-pole-diameter projectile accelerating to barely subsonic is searing. The blast is monumental, spraying flaming chunks of vessel all over the place. I told Mitch that a four-kilo PE4 warhead wrapped in motorcycle drivechains was a little over the top, but he insisted. Said it needed to kill and send a message.

We came out of the Eurowar with a lot of shiny new bodyparts. I've already called Turvey, our surgeon, and he's prepping a new lower torso. Guess I'd better sling the gear into the Landie and go evac Mitch, so I can deliver him and his legs to the bodyshop.

Treason and Plot

The national unrest that prompted the emergency session of parliament on November 5th 2053 can now be seen in the correct light: a massively and carefully orchestrated strategy.

At 13:57 a BAe Nightwraith stealth bomber was seen flying up the Thames estuary at near-supersonic speed and at an altitude of barely fifty metres. By the time an alert was raised, it was too late. The bomber unloaded its entire high-explosive payload into the Houses of Parliament with the accuracy this aircraft was famed for. There were no survivors and in the aftermath the lone Nightwraith escaped northwards, never to be seen again.

from Shattered Empires: The Fall of the Western Hegemonies.

Lunar Press Edition, 2088.

The mystery around that plane haunted me for years. The planning required to put the targets in place was almost inconceivable. But I always felt for the pilot. What drove him to volunteer for that mission? How did he escape?

I'm sitting in near darkness, listening to the wind howl and rain hammer at the doors of this semi-subterranean hangar. It was secretly constructed by roofing over and then extending a WW2 era Spitfire dispersal pen at long-derelict RAF Skeabrae in the Orkneys. Bracing my back is the perished remains of a Nightwraith front undercarriage wheel. Above me in the firelight looms the blue-black darkness of a piece of history. I could just make out the word 'Fawkes' stencilled on the port intake earlier, but the night has closed in.

In my mittened hand is a dead tablet computer I found in the cockpit. The words on its screen were written with acid-etch marker. I've read them so many times, but what to do with all this eludes me. So I read them again:

I have no idea when this will be found. The later the better, really. Governments like that I have just decapitated are useless against invisible opponents. Give them a name and their propaganda machines will make mincemeat of any cause. But give them ghosts and their paranoia will cause them to oppress their populations until rebellion occurs.

Who am I? A veteran pilot. Someone who flew missions in the service of the government I have just slaughtered. I did seek alternatives, but circumstances and evidence brought me to the decision I acted upon earlier today.

As for my name, so that I may be immortalised or condemned? No. Hopefully I am the one who has started a change, given others something to build upon. I am content with that.

Let me remain -

Anonymous.

I cannot encompass this. A selfless act, denounced as treason, that started a change in the way the western world was ruled. The realisation that a government had to be truly accountable. Fear of this Nightwraith and a greater fear of those who sent it was corrosive.

The only other remnant I found was a crumbling flight glove, under a panel in the Nightwraith's cockpit. Scored into the cuff, in the same hand as on the tablet, were three letters:

AMY

I sit here and imagine a darkened field, a terrifying stealth landing on a runway supposedly too short, followed by a wait, during which time the note was etched into the tablet. Then for some reason, a hasty departure, probably to meet a ship to take them out through the lochs. No time to hunt for a glove dropped in an out of the way place.

Where did you go, Amy?

With that question, I realise that my quest is not over. Tomorrow I begin again, this time with a heroine to find.

Duty

God what a mess. Twenty-one children, three mothers and eight staff dead.

"Come up with a cover story by midnight, Rog."

I look at my commander's departing back in horror. Cover this up? The man is insane. It's time to come clean, to let the public know. All that comes out of my mouth is: "Yes Sir."

The nanomachine revolution took us into a new age, giving every crazy benefit that science fiction writers had predicted and a few more, plus unexpected side effects. Under all the clever rhetoric for a new nano-enabled world, there were old habits. Tolerances were not fine enough, the full ramifications were not thought through. Nanomachines are part of our bodies and we all excrete nanomachines in our natural processes.

In every sewer across the world, under the effluent, a layer of nanite debris accumulated. Millions of tiny machines lay quiescent. A hacker named Karni discovered that this nanosludge could be harnessed, could be repurposed. She created the first 'packrat', a rodent infested with intrusion nanotech and malware. Pretty soon, any organisation with drains and conduits could be infiltrated. The response was predictable. Mahivista created the first cyberviper. It hunted packrats and when it bit them, it shorted out any nanomachines on board.

We expected the hackers to respond, but capturing and reprogramming cybervipers for assassinations was unexpectedly lateral thinking. NanSec produced the first enhanced mongoose within a year. But the instruction set that drove the mongoose was too easy to adapt. Pretty soon we were having to secure premises and people against a whole menagerie of enhanced animals with bad intentions.

Stefflin introduced HomeGuard last year. A sentry gun system that targeted any biological organism smaller than an adult human which had nanite enhancements and did not have a FamilyNet identifier. As FamilyNet implants had been mandated in all newborns for over two decades, the powers figured that any collateral damage would only be undesirables. The public accepted the spiel and the occasional dead waif is quietly cremated.

The Cybernary were formed nine years ago to police technologically-savvy antisocials. After five years of failures, we were given access to military technology and a new mandate that had two parts: the first being public, the second created for events like today's – a homicidal hacker sidestepping the stupendous encryption protecting HomeGuard installations by attacking FamilyNet units with an erasure program.

Every invitee had come to Timothy Stefflin's tenth birthday party. The clowns had just finished when the Stefflin's showpiece triple-redundant strategic HomeGuard system registered an infestation of small nano-enhanced bioforms without FamilyNet IDs. It went into purge mode and cleared the threat in under two minutes before alerting all the necessary authorities: the system conducted a massacre and then called in witnesses. Some murderous lunatic must have laughed himself ecstatic.

In the topiary and shrubbery at the edge of the estate a dozen difficult to see forms move purposefully at my command. A flash of white tail-tip and they're gone. One picked up a trace and all will follow it.

While Stefflin made a big fuss about HomeGuard and everyone signed up to the 'no more enhanced animals' treaty, Mahivista teamed up with GCHQ and made Flashfoxes. They have polymorphic camouflage, climb like cats, track data like wolves track blood, fight like wolverines and if that isn't enough, they can detonate like a kilo of RDX wrapped in nails.

Murderous lunatic is going to be dead by twenty-three hundred. Then I'm going to coerce Stefflin into admitting a 'psychotic disgruntled employee incident' by midnight.

Tomorrow I'm going to hate myself. Today I work.

Back to Me

I've forgotten something. It irritates me every day, being this world's oracle, yet knowing I've forgotten something important. Assassinations, disasters, discoveries: I have foreknowledge of them all. It's made several fortunes for many grateful and powerful people. Took me twenty years to realise that money wasn't what it was all about. Took me ten more to love a woman despite knowing the day she would die in my arms. When we know things are going to go bad, our first response seems to be fear. Overcoming that fear is what makes us human.

But every day I wake knowing that I've forgotten something. Makes me mean for the first hour of every day.

"Are you ready, Professor Daniels?"

Of course, being prescient with a greater or lesser degree of lead time, but always having the details, means I have placed myself well. I am sure that for every miracle I have laid claim to, there is a hard working someone out there cursing the fact that I beat them to it by a short period of time.

"I'm coming, David. Are we ready?"

Today I'm test-firing what those in the know have christened 'The Ghost Gun'. It's a large device designed to punch a hole in the fabric of our realities to let the user see events far away in space or time. Despite the excitement, especially at the temporal aspect, no-one wants the job of being the first 'prime voyeur'.

I walk slowly down the length of the bunker, admiring the huge machine that fills it. Twisting ducts laced with pipework surround a core that accelerates specific sub-atomic particles while simultaneously reining others back. The vision of this took me a week to write out and I am very sure that someone is going to be utterly confounded about how I got it done before them.

I lay in the recliner that contains the restrictors and let the accelerator web drop over me. With a thumbs-up signal to David, I ready myself to remember as much as possible of what I am about to see. I've chosen the Trojan Horse as my focal point. I'd like to be able to tell people what really happened.

"Happy viewing, Prof. Activating now."

There is a whine that escalates to a teeth-jarring howl as my chair vibrates like a massager gone berserk. I'm just getting nervous when a green flash blinds me and a voice speaks in my head.

"Welcome back."

I remember. Left-brain consciousness returns to right-brain me and I remember: I've done this before. So many times before. My prescience is only due to subconscious recollection of events I have lived repeatedly since I first sat in this chair. Every iteration I learn more and remember more, but every time I fail to recollect the one thing I really forgot, the flash of inspiration that came to me as I settled to sleep on the night before the first time, something that I had to do before I used the chair. A correction.

Or a modification. But I didn't write it down and forgot by morning, that fateful morning. I reach this point and know that this machine was truly my invention, but until I can recall that essential piece, I cannot figure out how to stop this. My brain's perfect lateral symmetry is possibly responsible for this repetition effect, but it makes no difference. Every time I come back to this moment, I know my chances next time round are worse. My right-brain consciousness really seems to travel back. But the left-brain consciousness remains. Each time we rejoin, I feel the slippage. My left brain consciousness has to wait thirty-five years in a sensory-deprivation limbo between moments. I'm going schizophrenic and beginning to suspect that I need my whole mind to have that key insight as I drift off to sleep.

The moment dies as the green light fades and I know I'll wake on the morning of my first day at college. It's my last whole thought. Goodbye, me.

The alarm sounds and I swat at it from under the covers. I need a few moments more. I'm sure there's something I wanted to remember.

Lesson of the Snows

The cave is warm and crowded. Eating is done and all present turn their eyes to the loreman when he rises to stand by the hearthfire, his shadow growing huge upon the rough hewn wall behind him. He turns full circle to regard all and everyone feels that they are his sole listener. That is why he is the loreman. He is the bard, his memory the history of all. He alone has done the seven year walk, visiting every tribe to listen to their stories. Tonight he tells a history woven from those threads.

"Listen well and hear the lesson that the snows whisper. Our forefathers conjured demons to do their bidding. Great cities of unnatural rock spread over the land whilst our forefathers flew above in carts that challenged eagles for mastery of the skies.

They harnessed demons into constructs that provided whatever the user demanded without the touch of crafter or smith. While these dark utopias spread, our forefathers lost touch with the land as their demon minions removed the need to heed unto nature.

Time passed and in their greed they strove tribe against tribe in terrible battles that turned good land into the night-blue crystal lowlands and reduced forests to ash, striking down cities with greater ease than we tear down termite mounds, and with less regard.

In the end our forefathers withdrew to the mountain vastnesses, building themselves great underground palaces in which to abide until the demon taints had been quieted by weather and time. But in their fear, they set about these havens armies of demon guards to protect them. They were still so fearful of other tribes that they forgot to defend against the little ills that even our children know to protect against.

It is said that a pestilence rose amongst them and the dying was an evil thing to behold. We know that the founders of our tribes were those who evaded the demon guards surrounding these places as they fled - guards turned merciless in the absence of overseers lost to disease.

In those palaces are the seeds of all that is needed to start again, to heal the blights upon the land, to calm the icy wrath of the sky.

The demon guards have outlived their masters, yet are still bound to their duty. Until they fail, we can only look upon the sites of these hidden citadels from afar, in wonder and despair. Our salvation is waiting but the sins of our forefathers are not yet expiated. We must survive this land of seven-moon winters until we are forgiven for the arrogance of our ancestors."

Eight Below

1: Consequences

"You, sir, are a disgustingly smug squid."

"Technically I'm an octopus, dear boy. But smug is indeed part of my ambience today."

"Pedantic, too. Exactly what did you expect to achieve by throwing Sir Ralph Bottomley through his new stained glass window?"

"I felt that if one is to defenestrate someone, one should do it with a certain style."

Jervis Merton sat back in his recliner and regarded his best friend and business partner from the world of Benthus. What on Earth caused these eight-legged starfarers to adapt so well to human society? In the hundred years or so since diplomatic relations commenced, the Benthusian Diaspora had resulted in them becoming ten percent of the population on damn near every human world, except for the few which maintained a xenophobic stance. The inhabitants of those planets seemed to be particularly offended by the 'Calamari Infestation' as they termed it. The Benthusians ignored those worlds and the diatribes that their representatives were prone to engage in if Benthusians were present at any event they attended.

His thoughts were interrupted by the sight of Hal stretching a tentacle to snag a fat cigar whilst simultaneously retrieving the table lighter, an ashtray, a snifter of rum and a cookie from the Wedgewood plate. Jervis shook his head and smiled as his unlikely friend settled himself deeper on the settee, shuffling cushions dextrously without spilling his rum or scattering crumbs as the cookie vanished into his beak.

"You may have exhibited 'a certain style', but did you have to practice it on the man with whom our sponsor is currently engaged in a vicious land-rights battle with?"

"Sorry, dear boy. The moment came and the man presented himself. Such a boor."

"Agreed that he is a prig of the first water. Which does not remove the problem raised by his untimely descent into a weed-clogged koi pond."

"I would have thought him thankful. Such leniency in landing was not part of my intentions. He insulted me and as such an unfortunately bad landing would have been legally acceptable."

"Not from three storeys up, old octopod, not from three storeys up."

"Hmmm. Fair point. But he seems to have taken it rather well. I was expecting lynch mobs and fiery rhetoric. All we have seen is a caution from the magistrate and a bill for his damnable window. They should be paying me; it was an awful piece of art."

"The quality of the work does not detract from the fact that it was on the obfuscated side of a building that stands in his private grounds."

"Are you trying to make me feel bad for tossing a bullying fop through a window, ostensibly to his doom?"

Jervis sighed. It was not like he disagreed with Hal. Sir Ralph did indeed deserve a bad end. A family fortune inherited from hard-working grandparents, doubled by a brutal father and quadrupled by Ralph who had not inherited one whit of the scant family morals or decency.

At that moment, a metallic clattering started outside the window and Jervis felt his ankle grabbed and then vigorously pulled by one of Hal's tentacles. He slid unceremoniously onto the carpet under the piano where Hal was already flattening himself as the clattering resolved itself into the opening rotations of a Gatling cannon. The barrage lasted for several minutes and completely devastated Jervis' home. The roaring silence after the Gatling spun to a standstill was punctuated by a single rough voice.

"You gutless calamari lovers and your eight-armed evil have three days to quit town. You can tell Miss Hawthorne that Sir Bottomley only said three days so she could depart like a lady, or as near as she can manage."

The sound of hooves and cart wheels rattling off down the cobbled street faded to silence. Under the table, Hal retrieved an undamaged cigar and lit it before turning a dark eye toward Jervis.

"Very well, Mister Merton. I now concede your point regarding unwise actions. So what now?"

Jervis rolled over carefully and tipped the remains of the rum from the ruins of the crystal decanter into his glass.

"I'd be minded to fight them and so would Miss Hawthorne. But we don't have the gunhands to do it and you're not exactly combative, being Benthusian gentry."

Hal nodded, a move that Jervis still could not fathom how he achieved.

"I am agreed. However, I am not without funds and more importantly, I do believe I can resolve the gunhand problem without resorting to gunsels. I just don't hold with paid pistoleers."

Jervis waved for Hal to pass him a cigar and the lighter. They lay on the floor in the ruins of his home for a while, sharing the moment of savouring that first smoke after near death. Finally Jervis hooked his arm under his head and turned his head to Hal.

"How can you fix it?"

"My brother Cal took a different route to the stars, paddling away from home just after puberty and taking one of the first luggers out. He's wandered across most of inhabited space in the last fifty years. He always drops me a stargram when he settles anywhere. Right now he's a Thurium miner on Banjax Nine. I can send him a 'gram and arrange fast passage. He could be here the day after tomorrow."

Jervis started. Those sort of interstellar transit times were exclusive to bonded couriers and the military. To ship a sentient by those means would involve costs that made him feel nauseous. He regarded Hal with a level gaze.

"You've not been entirely straight about your background have you, Mister Lamarry?"

Hal paled and then blushed crimson.

"I may have been a little vague. My bloodline is quite highly regarded on Benthus."

"How high?"

"I believe the human term for my kin is 'Honoured'."

Jervis sat up so fast he slammed his head into the underside of the piano.

"You're octopod ROYALTY?"

"Please. Not so loud. It's not like I'm due to succeed to the throne anytime soon."

"Succeed? You mean that you are direct lineage?"

"Oh good grief no. Cal is before me."

Jervis lay back down again. The implications of accidentally getting one of the heirs to the Obsidian Bier killed in a pissant disagreement over land-rights was enough to make his head spin.

"Jervis? I trust you are well?"

"Ye gods, Hal. Next you'll tell me you could buy this planet to stop Bottomley."

"I could, dear boy. But that's not the point, now is it?"

Jervis extricated himself from under the ruined piano and sat up, rubbing his head.

"You're right. Bottomley needs his sadistic backside handed to him properly. So why is Honoured Cal such a good option?"

"Please. Just Cal. He will kill you if you address him formally. From what we have heard and from the Benthusians that have come across him, or indeed opposed him, Cal has become somewhat of a force for justice, when he's not indulging his penchants for gambling, wine and human women. He is called '*plectredda lobai trune*' by those who have seen him fight."

"Plek-tredder what?"

"The closest I can translate it to is 'eight limbed star of death'. It seems my brother, to use your idiom, is 'rather tasty' in a fight."

Jervis smiled. Things just might work out non-fatally after all. Hal lifted himself and ruefully slid a tentacle tip through the sizeable hole in his retrieved topper.

"I do believe that I shall stargram Cal immediately. Your telegraph is in the kitchen, is it not?"

"It was." Jervis sighed as he regarded the chipped, splintered and shredded remains of his home.

"Fear not, dear boy. All shall be replaced or repaired and those who dealt this will be brought low. My brother acquired another name from assisting in a similar incident that befell one of my uncles. The indigens there called him '*Doothic vermanda*'."

"Do what?"

"It translates directly: 'Nasty bastard'."

"Now I am actually worried about meeting him. Thanks."

"No worries, dear boy. I'm sure you'll get along famously, but just to be sure, could you get the name of a quality brothel that welcomes my kind and serves decent tequila?"

Jervis stood stunned as Hal ambulated from the room, barely disturbing the debris. All of a sudden and a tad too late, he had serious reservations sliding through his mind.

2: Memories

*** RUSH URGENT TO: MISTER CAL LAMARRY, 8 BLOCK, ESCLATT, BANJAX 9 ***
Cal. I have heard the words 'eight-armed evil' again. This time from an agent of one who is opposed to me and mine. There is blood in the waters, dear brother, and sharks of hatred drive the shoal that surrounds me. 75 hours before Maquada becomes my final dive. With regret, I must call upon you again. Hal.
*** RUSH URGENT FROM: HAL, MERTON INVESTIGATIONS, 9 MAIDEN CLOSE, FARGONE, EDENLAND, MAQUADA ***

Cal settled his duster over his poncho and strode toward the upship ramp. He had said his goodbyes, and despite many promises, knew that his time here was done. Hal calling upon him was not the deciding factor, it was the mention of 'eight-armed evil'. That term had haunted and driven him for three decades.

She had been everything that he thought it impossible for a human to be. Theresa, Lady of House Solingen, daughter of Amadeus Solingen, the renowned weapons baron. It had meant nothing to the mob that had firebombed their home while he was away on business for her father. Her father had only narrowly escaped with his life and his second wife. They were the only survivors. Theresa and twelve staff had been burnt to death.

Since then, Cal had spent his life travelling the stars and extinguishing those who served the Brotherhood of the Reef, a secretive organisation with an extreme anti-Benthusian agenda driven by some obscure, quasi-religious ideals from Old Earth. Most of the time, it amounted to no more than a fancy club to practice bigotry amongst like-minded idiots. But every now and then, Cal had encountered and killed a zealot with more than just excuses for xenophobic bullying behind his actions. From them and with discrete enquiries, he had discovered that the Brotherhood of the Reef hid a fanatical core, a group of humans with nothing less than the annihilation of Benthus as their goal. He had spread the word and was now backed by a small group of equally deadly and dedicated scion of Benthus. They all roamed the star ways as octopod vagabonds, but wherever they landed, the torch of the Brotherhood was soon extinguished.

With a shake of his head, he passed through exit checks and onto the military courier on which Hal had purchased passage for him on. He used his family ties just once, to send seven terse stargrams in Benthusian by the fastest means to a half-dozen locations. With that, he settled into his sleeping vat and went promptly into an ink trance.

3: Hot Lead and Cold Steel

Miss Eleanor Hawthorne was a lady in all things. From smithying at her stables to discussing lace patterns with the dowagers of the Women's Company, she radiated a genteel calm. Thus, it was more than a little disturbing for Jervis to hear her curse like a stardock navvy as she kicked a gunsel squarely in the gonads with everything she had behind the elegant riding boot that protected her delicate toes from encountering the vagabond's privates. Said gunsel emitted a truly awful scream before collapsing. Eleanor crouched by the gasping and crying form while she reloaded. She paused after two shells, shot him in the face and then calmly continued to reload as bullets whistled about her.

Jervis slid himself further under the hardware store's porch and shot another would-be sniper through a window in the railhead hotel. Bottomley's gunsels were headquartered there, and had demonstrated surprising brains amongst their usually brutish number by actually making provisions in case their outnumbered opponents tried a pre-emptive strike.

Which was unfortunate for said opponents when they tried just that. Despite Hal's counsel to wait for his brother, Eleanor had insisted on trying to resolve the situation directly without outside interference: "Damn it,

Merton. We take care of our own troubles around here. You should never have agreed to Hal sending for his brother."

His reply had fallen on deaf ears: "They took a Gatling cannon to my home, Eleanor. That sort of vicious is beyond the trouble we usually deal with ourselves."

So here they were. Admittedly it looked a lot worse than it was, as Eleanor's gunsels were being led by her gunhands around the back of the main street, through the paddocks to the far side of the railhead hotel. While they did that, a few folk needed to keep Bottomley's gunsels distracted. That fell to Eleanor, Jervis, Hal and half a dozen of their more intrepid friends. So far, it had been going as expected. Which meant they were pinned down, sniping and skirmishing with the occasional gunsel who forayed out to test their mettle.

Hal was higher up, being on the balcony of the saloon next to the hardware store, using his advantage of limbs to keep a double thickness of tabletops between him and the bullets. His pistol was a Benthusian Magnum, a death-dealing weapon renowned across the whole of inhabited space. Jervis had reluctantly concluded that although it was a significant cannon, it was only legendary in the tentacles of an octopod who could actually shoot.

"Jervis, dear boy. Still alive?"

"Indeed I am, Hal my old octopod. How fares the reputation of Benthusian gunhands?"

"It fares poorly in my inept clutches, I regret to say. Although the amount of ducking and diving I cause when I fire is a small consolation."

"Do you two happy chaps want to stop having a convivial chat and get down to shooting some more bad men? In your case, Hal, just fire in their general direction."

The shout from across the way indicated that Eleanor's genteel had finally fallen off completely. Hal replied without rancour: "Certainly, dear lady. I do believe they are about to try something new. Look at the roof."

The hotel's level roof was four storeys up and covered with the usual blocks and tubes of utility and function. But some of them were clearly hides for bad things. With a clattering roar, a Gatling cannon hammered down. Due to the gunner's advantage of height, the next few moments were deeply unpleasant and spent scrabbling for some sort of substantial cover. Amidst his desperate attempts to avoid death, Jervis heard a louder roar from the direction of the paddocks. A twin Gatling cannon would cut their flanking movement to pieces. The paddocks offered no cover. It would be a massacre unless the gunner took mercy on his hapless targets. Jervis was just contemplating how unlikely that was when a Gatling round shattered his calf just below the knee. He screamed in agony and then swore vehemently when his body just would not pass out. Gritting his teeth, he had just resigned himself to being conscious for a bullet-riddled death when a monstrous explosion signalled the end of the railhead hotel. A cloud of smoke and dust rolled down the street, obscuring everything. Through the murk, Jervis saw Hal's distinctive shape ambulate rapidly down the side of the saloon into the steel waterbutt at the entrance to the alley between the saloon and the hardware store. A bubbling noise ended in a very loud hawking and spitting sound. Liquid spattered the ground by the waterbutt.

"Jervis, have you survived?"

"One leg down but still kicking, Hal. What the bloody hell was that?"

"I have no idea. One can only hope that they had a mishap with their ordnance."

"Amen to that."

The dust from the blast drifted west on the wind, leaving the main street clear except for the trails of thicker smoke wafting from the larger burnt remains. Fragments of the hotel and its contents plummeted back to earth, their impacts loud in the silence.

Gradually becoming visible in the clearing air, eight tall figures with wide, low set Stetsons stood silently in front of the railhead, their bodies shrouded in form-obscuring ponchos that hung to the ground and rippled suggestively in the wayward breeze. The one at the rear, on the side nearest the railhead hotel, had a lumpy projection from its silhouette; Jervis guessed that it was toting a massive force cannon of some kind, undoubtedly responsible for the hotel's demise. Meanwhile, the Stetson on the foremost figure rotated slowly, as if the being underneath were taking in the scene without comment or perturbation.

"Oh my."

Jervis rolled over to regard Hal, beak-deep in the nearby water butt. He dragged his wounded leg into a vaguely less agonising position and spat blood and dirt into the dust.

"What now?"

"It seems that my brother took my vague misgivings to heart. Unless I am delirious from dust inhalation, that is he, with all seven of my sisters."

"Is that bad?"

"For those who have attempted to harm me, indubitably. Do you have a cigar?"

"Why?"

"Because I wouldn't want to watch what comes next without one. Cinematic events deserve ritual trappings. I will admit that a snifter of rum is out of the question, but a cigar seems a reasonable compromise."

Jervis dragged himself to rest against Hal's water-filled refuge.

"Bottomley hired every gunsel on the continent. What can eight octopods do to challenge his army?"

"Watch and learn, dear boy. Watch and learn."

Jervis knew from conversations with Hal that Benthusians, despite having eight legs, rarely used more than two as arms. In extremis, they might use three or four. To see the leading poncho-clad figure bring up six tentacles, each holding a Benthusian Magnum, was a shock. The following exchange of fire with the occupants of the saddlery opposite the smoking ruins of the railhead hotel was vicious and very short. Jervis' intuition that a Benthusian Magnum was a formidable weapon in the hands of one who could use it was proven beyond question. He marvelled further as the creature sprinted into the ruins of the hotel, leaping nimbly like a human hurdler over the ruined walls, magnums blazing.

"Ah, brother dear. So good to see that you have not lost you touch."

"That was your brother?"

"Indubitably. There isn't another octopod in the universe who can manoeuvre on two limbs like that. He is a prodigy of Mother Hydra and the only male to be acknowledged by the devotees of that order. Speaking of which, that is Sal conducting open-vermin surgery outside the pawn shop. Tal is the one with the quadruple single-swords. I do hope you get to see her in action, it really is an art."

Jervis shook his head, the images before him assaulting his mind as four octopods using at least four arms apiece set about the stunned remains of Bottomley's gunsels with an assortment of very sharp implements. Two of the others unlimbered an astonishing assortment of rapid-fire projectile weapons, all seemingly loaded with ammunition that caused those hit to explode messily. Screams, blood and gobbets of gunsel filled the air as it became very clear that most of them were too stunned to even react in their own defence. Jervis could not suppress a smile after one of the sisters entered a boarding house across the way and all the noises associated with a low-budget film fight sequence in a building ensued, punctuated by battered bodies hurtling or flopping out of windows, a floor at a time. It really was something to see, although something he only ever wanted to see this once.

His observations were curtailed by Eleanor sliding under the porch next to him, bleeding copiously from a wound where a smallbore round had passed through her shoulder. He concentrated on staunching the flow and patching her up as best he could. By the time he had done, Eleanor was semi-conscious and the sounds of combat had ceased.

Jervis helped her out from under the porch and sat her on the steps of the hardware store before looking about. Hal stood to one side; four of his tentacles wrapped around four larger variants of the same that emerged from under the poncho of an octopod who overtopped Hal by half a metre. The Stetson lifted and two utterly black orbs held Jervis in a cold regard.

"Cal, this is Jervis Merton. The lady with the shocking bullet wound is Eleanor Hawthorne."

"Pleased to meet you. Excuse me: I have a Reefer to torture for information."

With that, Cal turned smoothly and ambulated off towards the paddocks. Jervis moved to follow when Hal restrained him with a pair of tentacles on his shoulder.

"You can barely walk and trust me when I say that you do not want to witness what is about to occur. Cal is rather single-minded regarding the Brotherhood of the Reef."

People were starting to emerge now that the battle was finally over. The owner of the saloon brought Hal a bottle of vintage rum and a clay pot with black leafed cheroots.

"Bless you, good fellow. Just what is required. I shall drop by tomorrow, if I may, and recompense you."

"Not a problem, Mister Lamarry. We all heard that it's your kin who are settling Bottomley's hash."

Hal's reply was interrupted by an impossibly loud gargling scream that cut off at midpoint. A poncho garbed figure peered around the side of the boarding house, a strangely shaped dripping knife grasped in the only visible tentacle; its voice was a soft soprano: "Apologies. We thought we'd gone past that. It won't happen again."

Hal waved a dismissive tentacle.

"Not a problem, Val. We understand."

Jervis turned to Hal.

"We do?"

"It's not like we can stop them, now is it? Far better we accept that bad things are occurring to a man who undoubtedly deserves them."

The saloon owner nodded sagely and returned to his premises to share the nugget of octopod wisdom. Eleanor's whisper reached only Jervis and Hal: "That's horseshit, isn't it? From my army time I suspect I know a bit of what's going on. Come clean."

Hal turned and regarded Eleanor and performed a little bow. He then folded himself down by her, so that his eyes were level with hers.

"I do not know for sure, but I suspect the use of the second or third Afflictions of the Father."

He regarded her steadily as Eleanor's complexion turned ash grey.

"You know far more than you should. That secret is safe with me."

Her voice was hoarse: "Poor bastard. No matter what he's done."

Hal nodded: "Indeed."

Jervis missed the rest of the whispered conversation as he saw Cal returning, accompanied by the seven sisters, three of them shaking blood from several of their tentacles. He tapped Hal gently with his toe. Hal rose and ambulated over to Cal. They had a rapid conversation in Benthusian before Cal turned and headed toward the railhead. One by one, each of the sisters twined tentacles with Hal and exchanged a few words with him before following Cal. As the last of them disappeared into the railhead, Hal turned and ambulated back to Jervis.

"Bottomley has fled offworld. The inner cadre of the Reefers are rightly terrified of Cal. For him to arrive with seven of the sisterhood sent Sir Ralph into paroxysms of fear. He chartered a flitter and up-shipped from Deuteronomy Field."

Jervis whistled. Fleeing three hundred miles to get the first ship out. That was a new level of scared. Then again, with something like Cal and his sisters after him, he'd be hightailing it offworld too.

Hal took a huge toke on his cheroot and chuckled, "He did make a very good point though."

"What's that?"

"Sir Bottomley's rather nice out of town residence is now vacant. I think that the new premises of Merton and Lamarry, Investigators at Law, are quite fitting for gentlemen of our standing."

Jervis laughed out loud.

"You just want to stop that damn stained glass window being replaced, you sneaky squid."

Hal rolled his dark eyes to the skies.

"Really, the very thought had not occurred to me at all, dear boy. Enough of the squidly insinuations too. Remember that I outnumber you by four and a half limbs at the moment."

Eleanor braced her shoulder as she shook with laughter: "He's got us, hopalong. Even with my help we can only muster six and a half between us."

4: Pursuit

Cal settled his duster over his poncho and wiggled himself down in the first class vat. A satisfactory and rapid saving of his sibling combined with getting within a single upship of a Reefer boss. A very good day's work.

"Brother. Are we pursuing this verminous human?"

"We are, dear sister. May I count on you for transport?"

"You may. I brought a fully cleared WidowStar as I felt something substantial might prove useful."

"You brought a WidowStar this far out? I presume the port authorities were very polite?"

"Positively unctuous."

The clicking and bubbling sounds of Benthusian chuckling filled the compartment as the train thundered through the evening.

The WidowStar may not have been the biggest of Benthusian warcraft, but it was without a doubt the blackest, in colour and reputation. Piloting the vessel required there to be at least ten limbs between the two pilots. It had variable geometry using a technology that even the Benthusians admitted was so esoteric that only a few of their scientists fully understood what enabled it. In full aggressive mode, the ship became a two-hundred metre diameter sphere of energy weapons, countermeasures and asymmetrical manoeuvring protrusions, all of which resembled truncated conical spikes of matte black material, patterned with intricate silver and pale blue designs that functioned as conduits, ornament and arrays. When not engaged in mayhem or retribution, the WidowStar could be configured to match the profile of virtually any ship in the hundred and fifty to two hundred and fifty metre class.

Fal had the ship shaped as an enormous, elongated teardrop. It sat in its own half-kilometre of clear space where local craft had actually repositioned themselves to be further away. Cal looked up at it as they strolled across the dusty apron. It had been decades since he'd ridden in a Benthusian ship. He felt a little tremor of delight. Despite vat design being standardised, he could always tell a vat made by a Benthusian from one made by a human.

"Brother. I have queried with donations to any human I accosted as you recommended and we are just this moment being supplied with the navigation plans of the ship that the Reefer scum boarded. We can arrive before he does. His definition of 'fast' is entirely deficient against a WidowStar."

Cal chuckled: "Dear sister. Against a WidowStar of the Obsidian Bier, everything not in high military use is deficient. I presume that this being a craft of the Bier, it is *fully* supplied to engage in aspects of hostility?"

"It is, brother mine. Fresh from my own pedigree tanks."

"Excellent. Let us go and introduce Sir Bottomley to some of our smaller brethren."

5: The Long Tentacle of the Law

Sir Ralph Bottomley was displeased. That was as far as he would admit to the bowel-clenching terror that had possessed him when he heard that royal calamari assassins were coming for him. Sitting in the executive lounge of the *Dixie Thunder*, he sipped a fine malt whiskey and regarded the single stargram he had received in reply to his hasty call for assistance.

*** RUSH URGENT TO: Sr R. Bottomley, CSP Dixie Thunder ***
You were advised against your actions in case they attracted Lamarry. So you took a Gatling to his partner's residence, burned his patron's businesses to the ground and started a land war. Next time, just tell us to butt out of your business and we'll go. There was no need to bring the possibility of discovery just to make your point.
I jest, of course. Do not expect a welcome anywhere, you idiot. Goodbye. KXV.
*** RUSH URGENT FROM: Sanders, CSW Mandate ***

After all he had done for the cause, they were abandoning him to his fate? Miserable lower-class ingrates, the lot of them. Fortunately he was not a stupid man and had engineered several ways to disappear even before he had been admitted to the inner circle of the Brotherhood. This rather hasty jaunt that was thankfully nearing its end was merely the first hackney en route to a leisurely promenade to the far side of human inhabited space on the finest starliners. Upon arrival he would take up residence amongst the calamari-free paradises that formed The Orcan Trade Union.

His daydream of a life of luxury amidst the formal gardens and mansions that were a feature of Orcan worlds was rudely interrupted by a polite cough from the white-gloved attendant who had arrived at his side unnoticed.

"What is it?"

"Sir Bottomley. The Captain respectfully requests your company on the bridge."

Sir Ralph's features broke into a smile for the first time in days. Much more as a gentleman should travel, invited to discuss matters of import with the Captain over a glass or two of what would, of course, be a fine vintage. He finished his drink, checked his appearance and then followed the attendant.

The bridge was far smaller than he expected, but his brusque querying of the uniformed officer he presumed to be the Captain was rudely interrupted by the jolt that paralysed him as he stepped through the doorway. His fall was prevented by the attendant, who deftly tipped him into a suspiciously convenient chair. As he sagged there, vigorously willing himself not to drool or soil himself, the officer he had sighted moments before stepped into his vision, a single piece of vellum in his hand. It was a medium strictly reserved for the transcription of formal diplomatic transmissions.

"Sir Ralph Bottomley. I am hereby ordered to restrain you as a precursor to handing you over to representatives of the Obsidian Bier. I am obliged to inform you that while you stand charged with multiple counts of fraud, affray, blackmail, extortion and incitement to murder on Maquada, all of these serious allegations have been placed in abeyance by order of the Supreme Justices due to prima facie and substantiated charges of attempted vaticide by proxy upon nine separate heirs and heiresses to the Obsidian Bier."

The officer raised both eyebrows and paused to stare at Sir Ralph as a shocked silence spread across the bridge: "Nine?" As a reply was impossible, he continued reading.

"Sir Ralph Bottomley. In accordance with agreements made, your estate and chattels are forfeit to the Obsidian Bier. Their disposition is entirely up to those you attempted to slay. This ruling also applies to your fate. May god have mercy on your soul."

The officer stopped, neatly folded the message and tucked it into Sir Ralph's top pocket. He then crouched down and stared Sir Ralph in the face.

"Reefers are an embarrassment to humanity. I am told that you are senior in their organisation. Now I don't expect you to understand, but they sent an honest-to-god Royal WidowStar to get you. A warship capable of taking on a whole fleet is hanging off my port bow. I can confidently say that you are going to die very badly and I for one am going to raise a glass to that."

He straightened up and gestured toward those out of Ralph's sight.

"Get this garbage off my ship. Put him and his goods in a transit balloon and let the Honoured on the WidowStar know that we are delighted to hand vermin like this over any time they want. Add our complete contact tags so they know we're available anytime if they call. It's not every day you get a chance to do a favour for Benthusian royalty."

He looked down as Sir Ralph was picked up by two crewmembers. His eyes held a knowledge that chilled Ralph to the core.

"Mercy is forbidden for those who attack the Obsidian Bier. You're going to be art before you're a corpse."

6: Justice is Served

Sir Ralph returned to consciousness after what he presumed had been a very long time. He could remember vague dreams of attending Brotherhood assemblies, regaling one and all with their efforts and plans, including the grand scheme at the heart of the Inner Order. He had answered questions with clarity and pride, the final solution to the Calamari Infestation never seeming so close.

He couldn't open his eyes! His attempts to touch his eyelids were also futile. He could feel his body, resting in what felt like a warm fluid. He felt his chin resting on something leathery and a soft material around his neck. He was just trying to remember his immediate past when a voice shattered his languor.

"He's awake, Cal. Brain activity is up."

Ralph felt tentacle tips on his eyelids, a prelude to them being slid open and secured by the pieces of tape momentarily visible in another pair of tentacles. He tried to look about, but his eyes were as unresponsive as his body. A familiar, terrifying form moved into his view.

"Welcome back, Sir Bottomley. You have been voluble during your rest. Be assured that your testimony will be instrumental in the utter destruction of the Brotherhood of the Reef."

Ralph's mind reeled in shock. His dreams had obviously been drug-induced interrogation trances. The damn Benthusian had pumped him dry!

"Brain activity indicates shock and anger, Cal."

"Understandable. To be outwitted by the eight-armed evil must be shameful to one such as this."

Ralph tried again to get control of his body, to no avail. Cal leaned closer, a tentacle curling into view. At the end, a small blue octopus rested, tiny tentacles wrapped around Cal's in a relaxed grip.

"This is one of my distant relatives. The scientific name is long and irrelevant to this moment. The common name is Statuemaker. They have a complex venom that induces complete muscular paralysis. It took us years to refine the dosage so that only gross muscular activity was affected. Autonomic groups still function. A paralysis so complete it is astonishing. I have experienced what you are currently suffering from, Sir Bottomley. It is quite terrifying, isn't it?"

The conversational tone was worse than the detail, not that Ralph could elucidate that.

Another tentacle came into view. The resident was another octopus, this one glossy black and held so its tentacles flailed. Ralph could hear the angry clicking of its beak.

"This is a Raximort. Its sole purpose is scavenging, the consumption of organic detritus. They travel in large groups, a living carpet of cleansing."

A vague misgiving started to form in Ralph's mind as Cal looked down.

"You are comfortable, I trust? The tank you are floating in is at just under human blood heat. On one side is a tube. At the end of the tube is another tank, where this Raximort came from. In a moment I will return it to its tangle. Then I will open the gate between the tanks."

Ralph tried to scream. He tried to flail. He tried to roll his eyes. Nothing happened. Cal moved back.

"The Statuemaker only causes paralysis. A complete lack of activity, like that of a corpse. The Raximort are hungry, having been starved for a while. These are cultivated for their serrated beaks and an appetite for Benthusian or human flesh."

Cal reached to one side and a faint splash broke the silence. His tentacles moved again and Ralph felt a vibration pass through the water he floated in.

"I expect this to take a long time. Excuse me while I follow the protocols."

Cal lifted a single plaque of obsidian into view, turning it so that Ralph could see the elaborate golden Benthusian cursives.

"Sir Ralph Bottomley, for crimes against the Obsidian Bier you are sentenced to be eaten alive by Raximort, the Sixth Affliction of the Father. This is deemed a fit tariff. You will be expiated when your last morsel has been consumed."

Cal lowered the plaque and Ralph felt little tentacles kneading the flesh of his thighs and buttocks.

"Good riddance, Ralph Bottomley. Die in agony."

As the first tiny beak tore into him, a scream started inside Ralph's head. It did not cease before his sanity left.

7: Hiatus

*** RUSH PRIORITY TO: HAL LAMARRY, C/O MISS E. HAWTHORNE, HAWTHORNE SPREAD, EDENLAND, MAQUADA ***
SRB was executed yesterday. Pick your fights more carefully, Hal. Next time I may be beyond swift intervention range. My compliments to your chap with the floppy leg and please extend my personal invitation to Miss Hawthorne to partake of a Benthusian spa sometime. Misbehave yourself, little brother. 2POBCI.
*** RUSH PRIORITY FROM: CAL, OBWS URCHIN ***

Hal looked up after reading out the stargram. Jervis had the rum decanter ready as Hal's empty glass lofted into view above the edge of the desk, shaking slightly in the outstretched tentacle.

Jervis poured and questioned: "I presume that the late, unlamented Sir Bottomley did not end well?"

"Correct. Forgive me if I do not dwell upon the probable details."

"Forgiven. What's a Benthusian spa? Eleanor was very curious and flattered in a vaguely discomfited way."

"As well she should be, my friend. It is something else I shall skirt the details of. Suffice to say it is a sexual activity practised by those of my race given to disporting with your kind. He really is quite disgraceful in mentioning it openly."

"Somehow I do not think that such niceties bother your brother. I also think that I shall present it to Eleanor as a mere scurrilous *double entendre*. Now what did those letters at the end mean?"

"There's more to the message. But the second part is coming by dedicated courier as the contents cannot be trusted to any form of remote communication. If Cal has chosen to use such extreme measures, we should be prepared for something of grave import."

That was what Jervis had feared. He sat back and took a cheroot from the humidor before spinning the table so Hal could reach. There was a moment's companionable silence, as they lit up and the first tokes were savoured, then Jervis pointed his cheroot at Hal to restart the conversation.

"How grave?"

Hal turned a rather vivid blue-green that clashed horribly with the burgundy of the settee he was draped on and over. Jervis shuddered and Hal chuckled: he knew Jervis' peculiar sensitivity to that sort of thing.

"It must be something directly related to this planet, dear boy. Something related to the Reefers' grand scheme as well. A combination that I do not relish, not one bit."

"I'll second that, old octopod."

"Nothing for it but to wait. I also think that we should turn our attentions to Bottomley's various concerns on this planet. I would guess that one of them is the root cause of this imminent message."

"Sound deduction, Hal. But for tomorrow, I believe."

"Agreed. Let us finish our drinks and adjourn to rest."

Jervis had barely risen to retire to bed when there was a pounding at the front door. He paused to retrieve and cock his pistol before moving to answer it. In the early morning gloom, a single figure stood on the stoop. The light coming over Jervis' shoulder picked muted highlights from the trooper's front-line battle gear and holstered weaponry. The man could have taken on most of Maquada without breaking into a sweat. He saluted Jervis sharply, heels clicking together with a metallic ring.

"Good morning Sir. I have an urgent personal message for Honoured Lamarry of the Obsidian Bier. Is he available? I can wait while he returns from trance, but I cannot impart the message to any save him."

Jervis was trying to find suitable words around his rum-abetted surprise when the trooper came to rigid, eyes-front attention and Hal's voice sounded behind him.

"Courier. Please enter and deliver your charge."

The trooper stepped past Jervis with an ease suggesting long practice. He bowed to Hal while offering a black tube with his offhand. Jervis noted the other had a ready grip on his pistol.

"Apologies, Honoured, but I must verify."

"Of course, courier." Hal wrapped a tentacle tip around the tube and it emitted a single chime. Hal looked over the trooper's bowed head at Jervis.

"Best to close the door, dear boy."

As the door closed, he heard the trooper whispering Benthusian with a fluency he had thought unattainable to human vocal capabilities. Hal stood, barely moving, until the trooper finished.

"Thank you, courier. Your charge is delivered. There is no reply. You are dismissed. Now can I offer you some refreshment?"

The trooper looked back at Jervis and blinked. Jervis came to his rescue: "This isn't your usual Benthusian royalty, soldier. Kitchen's down the left hallway and cook should be up by now. Take a moment before setting off again."

Hal gestured to the hallway mentioned by Jervis.

"Courier, would it help if I made that an order?"

The trooper nodded.

"Very well. In recognition of your commendable alacrity in delivering your charge, I order you and your pilot to take an hour or two to drink and eat. Tell him to park the patrol vessel on the lawn below the pond."

Jervis darted to the window to see a thirty metre vessel of sleek lines and angular plates descend smoothly to set down between the ornamental rockery and the rose garden without disturbing a leaf. He shook his head in amazement.

"Jervis, dear boy. They have to land with such gentle precision in the grounds of the Obsidian Bier. There are too many spawn ambulating about to ever be sure of a clear landing."

"Oh."

The trooper grinned at Jervis as he headed for the kitchen. "The little buggers are everywhere, sir. Have to check your boots and harness every morning for hitchhikers."

Hal's rear tentacles intertwined happily as the trooper disappeared.

Jervis grinned at him. "Homesick, old octopod?"

Hal waved two frontal tentacles in mock menace. "Perish the thought, dear boy. My home is anywhere I can clash with your décor."

"Thanks. Now, what was the message?"

"Tomorrow, Jervis. Let us go and bemuse the courier and his pilot for a while as I quite fancy some bacon before taking my rest."

"Sure?"

"About the bacon? Quite sure. As for the message, trust me that these few hours will be the last simple ones we enjoy for a while. Let us go and eat. Do you think we could inveigle chef into preparing Irish coffee at this disgraceful hour?"

"If you let him have one himself, undoubtedly."

8: Solutions

Jervis regarded the reporter from the Maquada Gazette with pity. He could never adequately capture the momentous events occurring here and he knew it. The excitement at being present was tempered by the crushing knowledge that his notepad was inadequate. Next to him, the news crew from Galactic Seven powered up their gear while glancing sideways at the local hack, sympathy in their gazes.

The room became attentive as Hal ambulated in, accompanied by a sizeable black Benthusian that seemed to radiate menace to Jervis' rather overwrought perceptions. He shot a glance at the G7 news team and they seemed to be aware of what they were seeing, and in raptures over it. One of them leaned over to the local cameraman and Jervis just caught the whispered advice: "Get some good shots of the black one. They'll sell like you wouldn't believe."

Hal clicked his beak loudly and the room quieted.

"Thank you for assembling here today. My companion is Arc Master Kul of the Zaferas. They are a contingent of Benthusians who wish for no contact with humanity. He is here purely at the request of Honoured Dal, Ascendant of the Obsidian Bier. He is only showing himself at my express request. Please note that any attempt to interact with him or any other black skinned Benthusians will at best result in severe injury. Am I clear?"

Nods and muttered assents were indispersed with covert glances between those present. What the hell was in the offing? The G7 news woman raised a hand and Hal gestured for her to continue.

"So this Zaferas group are your equivalent of the Brotherhood of the Reef?"

Arc Master Kul crossed the room faster than many people even saw. The woman was turning purple in a noose of tentacle before Hal barked a sharp, guttural phrase in Benthusian which caused Kul to drop her and return to his place with a similarly terrifying alacrity, ignoring the consternation he had caused.

"Members of the Zaferas consider that to be a mortal insult, madam. I regret that the object lesson arrived before I could explain. Could someone please summon medical attention for the correspondent?"

She was carried from the room while all present shuffled whatever they had to hand. When things had quietened down, Hal clicked for attention once more.

"Information gleaned from the late Sir Ralph Bottomley prior to his execution for crimes against the Obsidian Bier have given us the chance to finally eradicate the Brotherhood of the Reef. That same information has led us to believe that a significant weapons cache has been secreted in the highland marshes of Maquada. It is to this end that a force will be leaving Edenland tomorrow on a mission to find and eradicate this menace."

The local reporter cautiously raised his hand. Hal nodded in his direction.

"If members of the Zaferas dislike humanity so much, why are they here?"

Hal deferred to Kul who had raised a tentacle. With a thick accent, the Arc Master replied: "We hold no enmity for humanity. We merely believe that the Obsidian Bier is best served by a group of us remaining independent of human influence. But this Brotherhood of the Reef is a blight that if left unchecked could ruin all our futures. It must be excised. We requested that the Zaferas be allowed to reply to the Brotherhood's claims of ideological kinship with us by being the ones who erase them from history."

The room was silent. The words 'excised' and 'erase' told us all just how far this was going to go.

Hal ended the meeting swiftly after that, exhorting all citizens of Maquada to be alert for unusual activity, but to remain close to their homes and communities until this matter was cleared up.

As the room cleared, Hal caught Jervis's eye with a 'join me' twining of his tentacles. He nodded toward Eleanor, sitting off to one side. Jervis smiled, she had slipped in without him noticing. He limped over to her.

"Good morning."

Eleanor twisted and nearly punched Jervis before she recognised him.

"Stupid man. I told you that I was a little edgy."

"Apologies. Hal wants us to join him."

"Only if you stand between me and Kul. The woman he noosed came within a millimetre of dying, did you know that?"

Jervis had a sudden suspicion that Arc Master Kul had beaten Hal to the warning deliberately, knowing a demonstration would be far more effective.

In the assembly hall, a large assembly of Federal Rangers and Arc Warriors filled the place with the hum and clatter of combat preparations. Jervis noted that the Arc Warriors were all substantially smaller than Kul, although even blacker, if that were possible. Hal was at the back, where a quiet tent had been erected, a rather extreme measure that filled Jervis with foreboding. Inside the tent, nothing could eavesdrop. Which was a good thing as Jervis swore out loud and Eleanor nearly fainted when they saw the scene within.

Arc Master Kul stood on sheet of canvas, being vigorously rubbed down by a trio of Arc Warriors. His black colour was coming off in rivulets and patches.

Hal turned to Jervis and Eleanor, tentacles writhing happily.

"Dal, may I present the Honourables Jervis Merton and Eleanor Hawthorne? Jervis, Eleanor; this is my eldest brother: Hydra's Consort Made Flesh, Arc Master of the Zaferas, Ascendant to the Obsidian Bier, *Dahl Le'a M'harri.*"

Eleanor performed a full curtsey and Jervis dropped to one knee, bowing his head down to the other. What else could possibly be adequate before the ruler of the Benthusian Empire?

"Brother mine, do I detect some rehearsal?"

"None. They are simply that well-mannered here. It's one of the reasons I love Maquada."

"Very well. Please rise and excuse my brevity with you, but I have to be elsewhere, and right soon."

Jervis straightened. He smiled: "The perils of responsibility."

Dal chuckled as he turned to reach for an immense cloak proferred by a green-skinned woman. Jervis did a double-take so intensely that Eleanor punched his arm.

Dal turned back, one tentacle draped across the green woman's shoulders. He pointed toward her with two of his other tentacles as he spoke: "This is Alanna, a dear friend and one who is fully conversant with the more delicate details of this mission. She has my full authority."

Her smile was warm as she reached gracefully to take Hal's proffered tentacle. As she did so, Dal placed a tentacle tip between Hal's eyes.

"Unto you I entrust the First Speaker for Humanity."

Alanna grabbed Dal's tentacle from Hal's head. Shaking the royal tentacle gently, she admonished Dal in a laughing voice: "Oh stop being mean, Dal. You know Hal would rather die than let harm come to me. Now go and be regal with those who need it, you mutant squid, and let me sort this. Go. *Go*."

Jervis and Eleanor stared aghast as Alanna actually made shooing motions with her hand as she ushered the ruler of the Benthusian empire from the tent down an opaque tube toward his transport. As he ambulated from view, she turned back with a grin: "He's so concerned about giving the right impression as Ascendant. I keep telling him that he should relax, but I guess that'll take another century or so. Now; Hal said you had real Earl Grey tea. Where would a green-skinned demoiselle find that?"

Eleanor regarded Alanna's svelte pale green figure, wrapped in translucent blue-green silk over the briefest of G-strings. She put her hands on her hips: "I think we'll get some brought to us. You'd give the Women's Company collective heart failure."

Alanna looked down at herself, then looked up mischievously: "Would it be the nipples, the nudity, or the green, do you think?"

Eleanor laughed as she slapped Jervis again for staring: "In his case, the nipples. In their case, the nudity and the green."

Hal ambulated over and took Alanna by the hands again: "My dear child, how lovely to see you grown. I shall summon victuals, including the tea you desire, while you tell Jervis and Eleanor what is to occur."

With a nod to Jervis and Eleanor, Hal ambulated swiftly from view. Jervis took a seat and stared at where the tent flap had concealed his friend from view.

"He's damned upset about something. He only gets formal and brief when he's really put off."

Alanna returned from where she had retrieved a cloak. Jervis noted it was the same colours as Dal's, but fitted her perfectly.

"I think I can explain Hal's upset. The short of it is that sometime in the next week, we are going to have to incinerate several square kilometres of your highland marshes. The act revolts him beyond reason and he is torn between duty and preference."

Eleanor sat with her mouth opening and closing but no sound coming out. Jervis gathered himself quickly: "I presume that the weapons-cache motive presented to the press is a cover for dark deeds with worse reasons?"

"It is. The Brotherhood of the Reef found a rare fungus that grows only in the highland marshes of Maquada. Collected and refined, it is lethal to Benthusians and untraceable in salt water. Their 'grand' plan was to refine several thousand tons and poison the oceans of Benthus. For obvious reasons, we must stop their preparations. For other reasons, we have to ensure that such a genocidal threat ceases to exist."

Eleanor nodded: "The mere threat of such is something that cannot be tolerated by the Obsidian Bier. Humanity would be the same way about a similar threat. Except we would have greedy fools who would stash it in the hope of making a profit."

Alanna smiled: "Which are precisely the problems facing Dal. The Zaferas are the only ones who can be absolutely trusted to eradicate the threat completely. Their only loyalties are to Benthus and to the Obsidian Bier. This contingent of Federal Rangers is also drawn from units resident upon Benthus."

*

The flight to the highlands would have been far more enjoyable had Jervis not been worrying about the results of this mission. He had volunteered to accompany Hal because his friend was so obviously distressed.

"Our only advantage is that the Reefers have scared off every other inhabitant of the highlands."

Jervis turned at the sound of Hal's voice.

"But it will not be easy, prying these fanatics from their home ground."

Jervis looked at Alanna, his mind coming to a conclusion that he did not like one bit, despite it being the best option. In yet another moment of understanding, he realised that his insight was the other reason that Hal had asked him along. Between the two of them, Jervis had always been the one to make the ungentlemanly decisions, frequently performing them as well. Now he understood his friend's sorrowful disquiet; Hal could never ascend the Obsidian Bier because he did not have the ruthlessness to rule well. Moments like this only reminded him of it.

Jervis leant against Hal: "It's one of those uncivilised moments again, isn't it, old octopod?"

Hal rolled an eye to regard Jervis: "You are perspicacious as usual, dear boy. Your capacity for shocking violence to good ends is a thing that will forever be beyond me."

Jervis gestured for Alanna to come nearer.

"Hal tells me that the Reefers are sole occupants of the territory. I presume that your devices have located the fungus fields and Reefer havens?"

Alanna nodded: "We have. It will be tough work extricating them from their holes."

Jervis' expression hardened and Hal shuddered gently.

"Then we don't try to extricate them. Burn it all from the air. Why should we waste gentlemen in killing vermin? After the burn-off, we go in and mop up."

Alanna only nodded. She walked over to the Arc Chief and Ranger captain and held a brief conversation. They nodded. As she returned, both warriors nodded to Jervis. Hard solutions made decisively united fighting gentlemen, regardless of background.

*

The fires raged for two days. Explosions that indicated concealed refining laboratories or weapons caches broke the roar of flames with concussions, some of them substantial. Fifteen square kilometres of the highland marshes were transformed into a scorched quagmire that attracted scavengers from across the continent.

The Zaferas and the Federal Rangers handled the mopping up, being the only folk on Maquada with relevant experience. A month later, Alanna was ready to depart with the troops, the grand scheme of the Brotherhood of the Reef having ceased to exist, along with the entirety of its inner cadre. No survivors had been found and any remains had been left to the scavengers by unanimous decision.

She stood before the huge transport holding a small cylinder as Jervis and Hal approached. As Hal reached to take her hands, she wrapped one of his tentacles around the container.

"The marshes will resurge next spring. Take this and scatter the seeds into the waterways that feed the marshes. You will have *Palaghel* again."

Hal took the cylinder gently, rotating an eye toward Jervis as he did so: "*Palaghel* is my spawning bloom, dear boy. Purple hearted like the deep abysses around the islands of my home and white-petalled like the snow atop the mountains here. They are embargoed flora. Maquada's highland marshes will attract enthusiasts from across the galaxy."

He turned his full attention back to Alanna: "Dal?"

Alanna nodded: "He knew how the torching would affect you. He chose the bloom himself and ensured it was of minimal ecological impact for Maquada's ecosystems. He's forwarded grant of remission to the Supreme Justices."

Hal turned to Jervis, who noticed his tentacles were twining relaxedly for the first time in a month.

"Give me a moment, dear boy."

Jervis shook hands with Alanna and retired to a polite distance as Hal had a conversation in rapid Benthusian with her. As she finally turned away and strode toward the ship, Jervis swore he could hear the Women's Company heave a sigh of relief. Her presence had caused an eruption of terribly polite outrage which had been quite trying for all those deemed to be at risk from her exotic appeal.

Hal ambulated over to his friend, his tentacles weaving idly: "We should get some reliable folk to settle up near the highlands to prevent the inevitable poaching attempts and organise tours and suchlike."

Jervis laughed: "Glad to have you back, old octopod. Much as I see your point, I do believe that it can wait until we have caught up on our relaxation. Shall we head for home or swing on down to the dining hall for a well-deserved restorative or two?"

"Two, dear boy? I feel that many bottles will accompany the steaks nicely. Dessert will require a decent claret. Cigars afterwards will need rum, of course. Don't make any appointments for tomorrow. A gentleman's relaxation requires duration and effort."

"Only with you, old octopod. Before we begin, I should mention that I refuse to discuss your plans for that damn stained glass window until I am sober and possessed of a night's uninterrupted sleep."

"Perish the thought, dear boy. I hadn't considered the use of such underhand tactics at all."

A Few More

They say that the Yanks had Kid Rock playing during Desert Storm. I can see how that worked for them, the brash fusion of rap, country and rock making them feel like gods as their A10s swooped down to chop enemy armour to pieces. Wouldn't have worked for us: that sort of stuff is just not our cup of tea.

"Blue Leader, Blue Two. Contact at thirty-nine thousand, eleven o'clock."

Blue Two is Leanna Jones: she would have been a supermodel before the war rolled civilisation back to the twentieth century. I check my stupidly small scanner screen and sure enough there they are; a string of cigar shaped monstrosities surrounded by the pinpricks of escort fighters. Looks like a dozen Commissars with a double umbrella of Leoshins.

"Blue Flight. Blue Leader. Party at eleven high, ladies and gentlemen. Stow your sarnies and finish your tea. I expect the guestlist to be empty before we lose daylight."

"Blue Leader, Blue Eight. Please confirm empty guestlist."

Blue Eight is Thomas Meckland, our chaplain. A lovely chap who should have a rural parish somewhere with a congregation of genteel pensioners.

"Blue Eight, Blue Leader. Pray for them, padre. We have to make sure they get the message about IPI airspace being no-fly zones."

"Blue Leader, Blue Eight. I understand, but the Lord would task me if I did not at least ask for mercy."

"Blue Eight, Blue Eleven. That's noble of you, Tommy. Now get your Mjolnir out."

Blue Eleven: the squadron's Asatru and high priest, David O'Neill. As uncompromising a man as I have ever met. Lost his entire family, clan and coven when London burned.

"Blue Flight, Blue Leader. Now you've done the after tea chat, shall we go and show Ivan Chin that his Huns ain't welcome?"

"Blue Flight, Blue Three. Boss is dropping his aitches. Snap to, children."

Blue Three: Elaine Moore, high priestess and hereditary witch. Also a mean electronics whizz and built like all big women should be.

"Blue Flight, Blue Two. Afterburners for intercept and cut through only. Come up under the Commissars, knock 'em silly while the Leoshins faff about trying to hit us without hitting the fat birds. Then get topside and spread like a starshell to mop up."

Blue Two: Peter Simmons, my lieutenant. Should be a guitarist in a famous blues band. Instead, like all of us, he's stuck in this craziness. But he's rock steady all the time. If we used silly callsigns, he'd be something like 'Iceman'.

"Blue Flight, Blue Leader. Tally ho!"

I bring the stick back and hold it there until my Spitfire is pointed at the enemy formation. I know Blue Flight is behind me, four trios in arrowhead formation: leader in the middle, wingmen on opposite flanks, high and low. I also know that as I hit the burners and depress the accelerator, eleven other hands and feet are doing the same.

My Spitfire looks like a cross between a classic Spitfire and the Yanks' original Sabre jet. They are the fighter others dream of having. All because a bloke called Ross predicted that this war would roll on for decades, eventually removing all our high-end technical capabilities. So, eleven years before it all went to rack and ruin, he designed an air-superiority fighter for a world that didn't exist. Minimal tech, all proven and maintainable with the commonest parts. Emphasis on simplicity and resilience. Plus an absolute mandate to be beautiful, deadly and fast.

Cleverer people than me are still trying to fully comprehend Mister Ross and his incredibly accurate visions of the place where we have been for the last fifteen years. I just thank his eccentric brilliance every time I see a Spitfire Mark Fifty-two. The fifty-ones were the first and apparently the mark number came from the fact that Ross considered the Seafire Mark Forty-seven to be the ultimate evolution of the Spitfire. Queen Kate ordered that the Spitfire name be used once more as Britain was alone against incredible odds. Everyone agreed and a legend was reincarnated.

The world is a shambles and the Vory-Triad Alliance, that formed as communism and post-communism collapsed in China and Russia respectively, had the experience, organisation and ruthlessness to become the de facto rulers of a very large chunk of the Middle and Far East. The United States, already unstable, ruptured wide open as a number of Tong-related scandals implicated politicians and corporate bosses up to the highest level. President Kyle Martin killing his Vice-President while defending himself on live television stopped an attempted coup, but dealt a death blow to the American dream. They're still fighting a very uncivil war over there and it looks like it's going to become almost African in its generation-long tribal hatreds.

The remaining players are the Federated European Economic Community and the Canadian and Alaskan Domestic Alliance. Everyone else contributes to whichever side threatens them the most. Britain is leading the Independent Peace Initiative, where countries refuse to support the ongoing war, just defend themselves and help each other where geographically possible. We all saw what happened to Switzerland on the day that 'neutrality' became the new word for 'juicy, poorly-defended target'. If you want peace, you have to fight to keep the war out.

We are winning. More countries have joined in the last year than in the previous five and even CADA are making overtures to swing from a full war footing to IPI membership. Getting them will change the balance. Suddenly FEEC will be facing VTA alone and that will be over very quickly, one way or another.

Meanwhile, I have a country to defend.

"Blue Flight, Blue Leader. Good hunting, boys and girls. For the Queen!"

Their shouts make me smile and I hit 'Play'. The com fills with a proper anthem: Motorhead's 'Sex and Death'. Something to fire the blood as we lace Britain's skies with contrails of defiance once again.

Late

He said he'd be back for my birthday.

"Yari, are you sure you don't want us to come round?"

No, mother. All I heard before he left was how this Skywing would break my heart. About how interracial pairings didn't work. About how Stuart from across the hall would be a good catch.

"I'll be fine, mum."

"We love you, dear. It's for the best. Better you found out sooner rather than later."

Bitch. Even on my birthday she can't let it go.

Under the setting sun, the view from the vent towers is beautiful. They rise above even the citadels, letting the exhaust from the city blow out over the bay.

I remember the first time Curran brought me up here, fastening a harness about me before clipping it to his bodysuit. Then he took me in a feather-rustling, arms and wings hug before toppling the two of us off the tower. I screamed so hard. We fell quickly, past people in the citadels racing to their balconies to watch us smear somewhere below them.

Then Curran unfurled his wings and swooped under the Magistrate's Bridge, up into the last light of the sun. He loved me! Skywings, or Parasularnans to use their proper name, only fly connected when with their lifemates. Curran held both my hands as we careened a laughing path until a patroller politely asked Curran to stop as they were being bombarded with reports of a mad Skywing kidnapping a woman.

I remember Curran smiling at the officer while hanging in the sky with lazy beats of his wings as the officer leant precariously out of an aircar.

"She is my lifemate, officer. I would sooner die myself than hurt her."

I missed the officer's reply because of the blood thundering in my ears.

From then on, it went so well that we were both worried. His comrades accepted me, while my family shunned me. Then the news of a rebellion came and Curran had to go. He led a special forces flight: there was no way he could avoid it.

The wind is turning chill and the sun is going down. Oh, my Curran, what happened to you? No information is available and it's like the rebellion just evaporated, taking my life with it. Seven months without news.

With a sad smile, I lay my phone bracelet on top of my kitbag and furl the jacket he gave me gently on top of it. I can't get it dirty.

Three quick steps are all I need to swan dive cleanly off the edge, feeling the air rush past and scour the sorrow from me. For a few minutes, it'll be like flying with his memory. Then it won't matter anymore.

I'm travelling so fast that I have to squint to see the lights of the underpass waiting to illumine my smashed remains.

There is a sudden crosswind where one cannot be. Arms wrap me and wings turn my plummet into a boost for the soaring arc that fails to keep up with my heart.

His voice is warm in my ear and laughing. "Little girl, little girl. I was hoping we could have our lifemate ceremony on my homeworld, not on a spaceport airfield to save me from court-martial."

There are special pardons extended to lifemates who do spectacular, impulsive, illegal things like blowing an emergency hatch to powerdive fully-armed out of a military transport over a city to stop their suicidal lifemate - who thinks that he died because his messages were not delivered - slamming into the ground at terminal velocity.

I murmur my reply into our kiss. "Next time, don't be late."